GRAND TALLY

OTHER WORKS BY ROBERT WOLF

Non-Fiction

The Writer Within: A Thorough and Enjoyable Guide to Writing from Everyday Life

The Triumph of Technique: The Industrialization of Agriculture and the Destruction of Rural America

An American Mosaic: Prose and Poetry by Everyday Folk

Heartland Portrait: Stories and Essays from the Rural Midwest

Crazeology: The Jazz Life of Bud Freeman

Story Jazz: A History of Chicago Jazz Styles

Violence in the Holy Land: Witnessing the Conflict in the Middle East

Plays

Driftless Dreams

Ragnorak: The Doom of the Gods

Heartland Portrait

The Strike at Pullman

The Arms Dealer

GRAND TALLY

A True Account of the Recent Happenings
in Moosehead, Montana
and
New York City

By

Robert Wolf

Drawings by the Author

Ruskin Press
Decorah, Iowa 52101

Copyright © 2013 by Robert Wolf. All rights reserved. Except for brief reviews, no part of this publication may be reproduced or transmitted in any form or by any means, electronic or mechanical, including Internet, photocopy, compact disc, recording, or any information or retrieval system without written permission from the publisher.

1. Fiction 2. Satire

Ruskin Press
P.O. Box 10
Decorah, Iowa 52101

All characters appearing in this work are fictitious. Any similarity to any real persons living or dead is purely coincidental.

CONTENTS

CHAPTER ONE

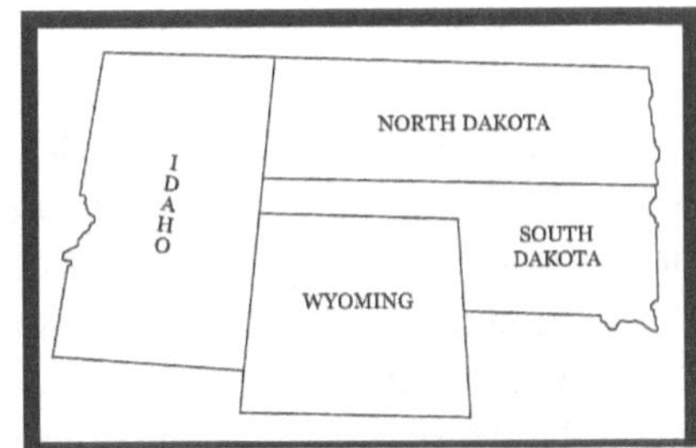

This narrative is the truth about the shootings in Moosehead, Montana, not what you probably read in the newspapers or saw on television. And the truth is that it was Grand Tally and no other group that was largely responsible for the violence that engulfed the FBI, the National Guard and the Montana militia.

Grand Tally, the company that calls itself "the world's greatest mapmaker," was founded thirty years before the American Revolution by Ebenezer Tally.

In time, Tally not only provided the most detailed and authoritative maps of the United States, but of every other country as well. Tally surveyors risked life and limb in the Congo, at the South Pole, in Siberia and Mongolia—everywhere. In these years the Tally Company renamed itself Grand Tally. Eventually, the *Tally World Atlas* became the most respected in the trade.

But all things change. By 1950, George Tally, great-great grandson of Ebenezer Tally, resigned as President and Chairman of the Board. His only son had no interest in the firm. The board appointed two Harvard MBAs, Leslie Driggs and Leonard Feinstein, to head the company. Neither Driggs nor Feinstein had any interest in maps, but as up-to-date businessmen knew that all that counted in making money was devotion to efficiency and proven accounting methods.

Thanks to their business acumen, Tally no longer employed cartographers. It no longer hired surveyors. Anyone with mapmaking expertise was hired on a project basis and worked at his own office, not Tally's. Grand Tally, "the world's foremost mapmaker," was now run by accountants.

2.

Inside Grand Tally offices on the seventy-fifth floor of a New York skyscraper, Jovina Rates, assistant accountant, sat at her desk examining the proof sheets of Grand Tally's new world atlas, its first in fifteen years. In a move designed to increase sales, Tally had combined its *U.S. Road Atlas* with its *Student World Atlas*. Newspapers and magazines were anticipating review copies.

The board of accountants, which had supervised the making of the atlas, had decided at the outset that the map would have 120 pages, no more or less. Ms. Rates was looking at the last page of the proof sheets for the atlas. Something was wrong, and she began to feel very sick. Her stomach began twisting itself into knots.

"Mr. Potts!" she called to a balding gentleman seated at a desk nearby.

"What is it?" Mr. Potts wanted to know.

"Something's wrong!"

"What's wrong?" insisted Mr. Potts.

"Please look. Come here."

Not very pleased at leaving his sandwich, Mr. Potts pushed back his chair, stood up and ambled over to Ms. Rates, who was jamming her left forefinger repeatedly onto the top left corner of the last page.

"What?" asked an irritated Potts.

"The number! The number!"

"What about the number?"

"Look!" she gasped in horror.

"For gawd's sake what?" insisted Potts.

"It's number one hundred twenty-two!" she rasped.

"It's a hundred twenty-two," Potts repeated emotionlessly.

"Yes! and the book's only supposed to have one hundred twenty pages." Ms. Rates slumped back in her chair.

Mr. Potts bent forward, turned the page over and said, "Did it ever dawn on you that this might be an error? Did you check the other numbers?"

"Yes," Ms. Rates answered quietly.

Mr. Potts began turning pages quickly, checking the numbers, moving from the last page to the first. The closer he got to the front of the book, the more agitated he became. At page one he decided that he must have missed a number and went from beginning to end, slowly. "A hundred twenty-two pages," he murmured when finished.

"Somebody's going to get sacked," Ms. Rates guessed.

"Not me," Potts assured her, "I didn't design it."

The two nervously notified their supervisor, who checked the book and called Henry Mason the vice-president for marketing, who checked it and called a meeting of his staff, which included Ms. Rates and Mr. Potts.

Mr. Mason and his staff discussed the problem, and as Mr. Mason said, "If there is one thing we have to base our decision on, it is the fact that the board of accountants made clear that this atlas is to have no more than one hundred twenty pages. Two pages have to go."

The staff looked at one another.

"The question is," said Mr. Mason, "which two."

Waiting for a decision from their leader, the staff looked at Mr. Mason.

"Well?" Mason asked. "What's your recommendation?" He scanned the frightened faces. "Ms. Duncan?"

Ms. Duncan's eyes moved back and forth as she glanced at her colleagues.

"Yes?" Mason asked reasonably.

"I—I don't know."

"Who," Mason asked, "has the leadership to make a suggestion?" He paused. "Remember, everyone's job is on the line."

"Why don't we combine some of the countries?" someone suggested.

"Good thinking," Mason said.

But it was decided that that would prove impracticable. So many pages would have to be shifted that the cost overrun would be enormous. And that, Mason knew, would get them all fired.

"What about removing some country?" someone suggested.

"Good God," someone else said, "can you imagine what that might mean for foreign sales? Besides, the world is so internationally oriented now that plenty of people would notice and we'd lose all credibility."

The group reluctantly agreed with this analysis.

"That pretty much leaves the United States," someone observed.

The logic of the suggestion was noted.

"So we cut out one or two of the states," Ms. Rates said.

"How do the rest of you feel about that?" asked Mason.

"I don't like it, but what choice do we have?" someone asked.

There was a murmur of agreement.

"How many of you agree with that?" Mason asked. "Let's see a show of hands."

Everyone looked at one another. A few began tentatively raising their hands, at which others began raising theirs. Soon everyone's hand was in the air.

"All right," Mason said. "We've reached a consensus. Now we need to decide which one or ones."

"Well," said Ms. Rates, "it's got to be unpopulated, whichever it is."

"Yup," someone said.

"One of the western states," a voice added.

Most of Grand Tally's employees had never been west of Pennsylvania, and despite the fact that they published a map of every state in the union, had no idea of what any of them looked like, let alone anything about their population or manufacturing or agricultural base. Moreover, they did not care. They were, to the core, hardline New Yorkers.

"South Dakota," someone suggested.

"What's that?" someone else joked.

"South Dakota's got Mount Rushmore," Mr. Mason said. "Too many dweebs driving out there to see the carved heads. Can't do it."

"North Dakota then," someone offered.

"Possibility," Mason said.

"No one lives there," Rates added.

"How about Wyoming?"

"Look for a western state that covers two pages."

Five employees scanned the pages of the proofs.

"North Dakota."

"Montana."

"South Dakota."

"We said no to South Dakota."

"I'd say Montana."

"Sounds good to me," someone said. "It's unpopulated, no one knows anything about it, no one cares."

"Let's take a vote," said Mr. Mason. "All in favor of eliminating Montana, raise their hands."

Everyone raised a hand. And so it was decided that Montana would be eliminated from the forthcoming *Grand Tally U.S. & World Atlas*.

"I've got one question," said Mr. Potts. "Do we tell Mr. Driggs?"

"I'll send a memo to Mr. Driggs telling him that we made an adjustment," said Mr.Mason.

That memo did not state that anything had been omitted, merely that two excess pages had been cut. Nor did it mention that in a moment of panic Mr. Mason, supported by a number of sub-accountants, had ordered the U.S. map redrawn to omit Montana. Mr. Driggs did not ask what had been cut. And that was that.

Two months later the *Grand Tally U.S. & World Atlas* was selling in every gas station across the United States.

3.

That summer Mr. and Mrs. Travers were crossing the western United States from Chicago to Montana in a large station wagon. Charles Travers was a chemical engineer with a slight paunch and a balding head. Mrs. Travers, overweight and asthmatic, sat in the front passenger seat. She was wearing sunglasses.

Mr. Travers had pulled the car over to the side of the road

and was staring unhappily at the desolate landscape.

"Damn it," he said, "we're lost."

"How can we be lost?" Mrs. Travers asked angrily. "We're on Highway 25. You said that goes all the way to Billings."

The Travers were headed for Moosehead, Montana to visit Mrs. Travers' brother, Buck.

"Only you could get lost," Mrs. Travers added.

Mr. Travers scowled at her, then said, "Cut the crap, Olivia."

"That's a fine way to talk."

"Where's the atlas?" he asked, ignoring her remark.

"Wherever you put it last," his wife informed him.

"For chrissake just cut the crap, Olivia, and get the map."

"Not when you talk like that with that tone of voice," she shot back.

Mr. Travers groaned and unbuckled his seat belt, got out and opened the back door. He rummaged around under the blankets and other items strewn about the back seat. He cursed his wife, the trip, the heat.

"You probably put it with the suitcases," said Mrs. Travers, becoming increasingly annoyed.

"Goddammit," Mr. Travers said as he shut the back door and headed for the back of the car. He found the atlas under the suitcases. By the time he got back in the front and buckled himself in, he was sweating.

"Here, give me the map," his wife said testily, and pulled it from his hands.

Mr. Travers exhaled loudly.

Mrs. Travers flipped through the pages. "Well, where the hell's Montana?"

"We're probably in it," Mr. Travers replied.

"Not that! Where's the map of Montana?"

"In the atlas," he replied sweetly.

She was flipping wildly through the pages. "It's not here!"

Mr. Travers smiled complacently. His wife was now looking for the index.

"Can't find Montana, huh?"

"Here," she snapped, "you find it!" She threw the atlas at him.

He looked at her darkly, then began flipping through the pages till he came to the United States, then looked for the states beginning with the letter 'm.' He found them: Maine, Maryland, Michigan, Minnesota, Mississippi, Nebraska. . . He turned back through the pages and looked, then looked some more.

"It's not there, is it?" Mrs. Olivia Travers said triumphantly.

"Got torn out of the book."

"Doesn't look like it. Forget it, just drive. Drive to the next town."

"That could be fifty miles."

"I don't care, I'm tired and hungry."

Mr. Travers put the car into drive and started off down the road.

4.

"Where do you suppose Olivia is?" asked Buck Simpson. Buck was sitting on a straight backed chair on his front porch, resting his booted feet on the rail.

"Hanged if I know," replied his wife, who sat next to a small table with a bowl in her lap and a pile of string beans on the table, snapping them.

"They should've been here by now," Buck complained.

"It's a long drive from Chicago. I wouldn't worry."

"When was they goin' to start?"

"Tuesday."

"Well, it's Friday now."

"They'll be here."

"We'll have us an ass-kickin' good time when they get here."

"We shore will, Buck."

"I wanna take them down to Sidewinders so they can do some dancin'. Think they'll like that?"

"Who wouldn't like dancin' at Sidewinders with a band like Buster Butts and His Eightballs."

Buck took another pull on his beer bottle. He grinned and shook his head approvingly. "We'll have us an ass-kickin' good time." He took another pull, then said, "Lorene, honey, would you get me my pint of bourbon?"

"Where is it?"

"In the broom closet, where I keep it."

As Lorene stepped inside, Drover Lankney, the postman, roared up in his pickup, stopped a moment at their mailbox, threw in a bundle of letters and magazines, honked his horn and roared off. Buck followed the cloud of dust Drover's pickup made as he tootled down the gravel road.

Lorene came out with the pint of bourbon.

"Sweetie pie," Buck cooed, "Drover's just come by with the mail. Since yore already on yore feet, would you mind gittin' it?"

Lorene stepped off the porch and headed for the road. Buck watched the swing of her rear end as she walked. After fifteen years of marriage, he still liked the swing of her rear end. He was still studying it when another pickup raced down the road, slowed at Buck's drive and pulled in. George "Cap" Matlock and Byron Pulver stepped out and walked over. Buck could tell something was wrong by the fact that the two were not ambling as usual, but walking with a quickened pace.

"Buck!" Cap called out, holding something like a book or magazine in his hand.

"Yo!" Buck shot back and took his feet off the rail and stood up.

"Somethin's up," Cap said.

"What's up?"

"Sheriff Brandt's locked up Lew Mitchell," Byron almost shouted.

"What?" Buck asked in disbelief. "What for?"

"For pissin' on his own property," Byron snorted. "Can ya beat that?"

Just then Lorene stepped back on the porch. "We got bills," she said.

"What else is new? We're talkin' about somethin' important," Buck told her.

"Pissin' on his own property," Byron repeated, then said, "Hello, Lorene."

"Hello, Byron. Hello, George. You fellas want somethin' t' drink?"

"No thanks, Lorene," Cap said.

Buck said, "Lew Mitchell's got arrested, Lorene, for pissin' on his property."

"That don't make no sense," Lorene said. "Any one can pee on his own property."

"Well, not according to the kind of law we got around here," Byron said.

"I don't believe it," Lorene said.

"Well, there was more to it," Cap said, gesturing and waving the magazine, or whatever it was.

"I thought so," said Lorene. "What's the real reason?"

"He took a shot at some guy who came a little too close to his property."

"Well then he ought to be arrested," Lorene said.

"It was his property," Byron insisted.

"George just said the man was not on Lew's property," Lorene replied. "Lew's a nut case. Serves 'im right."

"He was just warnin' the guy off," Cap said.

"Wasn't reason enough to lock 'im up," Byron countered.

"Lorene," Buck said, "do you mind? Let us handle this."

Lorene turned and walked back inside the house.

The men looked at each other. For three years they had grown increasingly suspicious and eventually hostile to any form of government. They no longer believed that county, state, or federal governments had any legitimate authority.

"Well?" Buck asked. "What do we do?"

"We're goin' to round up some of the boys and talk about it," Cap said. "Better come along. And another thing, look at this." He held up a book, a magazine, or something.

"What is it?"

"The new *Grand Tally U.S. & World Atlas*. It don't even got Montana in it." Cap opened it up. "Try to find Montana."

Buck tried and failed.

"Now look at this."

Cap took the atlas and opened to the U.S. map.

"Try to find Montana on this."

Buck looked and saw four grossly enlarged states—North and South Dakota, Wyoming, and Idaho—swallowing up what had once been Montana.

"What the hell is this?" he said in disbelief. He closed the atlas and looked at the cover. "Grand Tally?"

"Yep," said Byron.

"What the hell is goin' on?" Buck wanted to know.

"I'll tell ya what I think it is," said Cap. "I think Grand Tally got hold of some government plans to do away with Montana and decided to go ahead an' publish them."

"Holy shit." Buck was stunned.

"There's gonna *be* some shit," said Byron.

"We gotta do somethin' t' make sure this"—waving the atlas—"doesn't happen."

"Okay," said Buck. "Lemme tell Lorene I'll be leavin'."

Buck opened the screen door, leaned inside and shouted, "Honey, I'm leaving with Cap and Byron. Be back later. Save my supper."

And the three of them were off.

5.

Agent Spencer Hardwicke of the FBI was known in the bureau for his fast, hard-hitting, on-the-field decisions. Hardwicke headed the bureau's domestic anti-terrorist team and this year he had overseen a standoff with a cult in a desolate region of Idaho. He was sitting at his Washington desk across from the FBI's chief standoff negotiator, Bill Rodney. The two men had worked together at the Idaho standoff, where the FBI, ATF, the Army National Guard, the local sheriff's department, and the Air Force had surrounded a shack where five members of the Brotherhood of the Aryan Light had declared themselves and their fifty-eight acres a sovereign nation.

Each day the bureau's anti-terrorist work was becoming more difficult as the bureau logged more and more reports of disaffected individuals and groups throughout the country. When he had first joined the bureau in the seventies, Hardwicke's few concerns were civil rights activists like Martin Luther King, Jr., the KKK, communist spies, editorial writers and commentators who had some gripe or other with the government, loners who occasionally called in bomb threats to metropolitan newspapers, and the personal enemies of the bureau's famous director.

Now he was dealing with white supremacist organizations, cults of all descriptions, anti-abortion groups that bombed clinics, a hundred militias, homo rights activists, Black Muslims, the Anti-Defamation League, and so many more he couldn't begin to list them. Besides these, and even more dangerous, were the Arabs living in the United States, tens of thousands of whom were actually citizens. But besides the Arabs, there were all the other Muslims—Pakistanis, Afghanis, and so on. How many of them were now U.S. citizens, or had snuck in illegally? It took the FBI's main frame computer a full week to print a complete list of suspected domestic security risks.

Out in the Western states Holbrook had to worry mostly about the militias and white supremacists. Most of these were property rights fanatics who hated zoning or any other local, state, or federal restriction on what they could or could not do with their property. The area around Moosehead, Montana was peppered with white supremacists and militias—a powder keg ready to explode—and he had two agents in Rosebud County alone, monitoring their activities.

6.

Hardwicke and Rodney were both interested in another group, the Remos, a charismatic Christian sect that handled lizards, went into trances, and was waiting for the Day of Judgment. Because they spoke in tongues they had come under the surveillance of the FBI after a bureau secretary had seen their leader, Enoch Angle, on local television news in Dubuque, Iowa, every square inch of him covered with lizards as he shouted praises to the Lord and called down the wrath of God on Satan's playground, America.

Angle was a tall, almost emaciated figure with a shaved head who claimed God spoke to him daily and had revealed that the end of the world was coming on July 31. This, Angle said, could be proven by reference to the Book of Revelation, and he tried to convince local ministers and priests of this, but not one cared to listen. The news media, however, were very interested. Newspapers and television stations occasionally sent writers and cameras to the group's downtown home, and Angle and his followers would describe the Wrath of God and the flames and droughts and winds it would soon call up. So much could be culled from the few intelligible sentences wedged between the torrents of sounds that tumbled out when the Remos spoke in tongues.

Jesus Christ, Enoch announced, would return three days before the End to call the faithful to his fold. He would rematerialize in a small town out West—just where God had not said, but He had instructed the Remos to take to the road and trust in His direction. The day after Angle announced that to reporters, the story ran in almost every major daily in the country. The networks ran thirty second pieces on the evening news, including interviews with cult experts who discussed whether the Remos posed a threat to themselves or others. The air waves were filled with speculation on such questions as whether or not they were likely to commit suicide if their leader's prediction proved untrue. Or would they instead turn on others? Should they be put under protective custody? Should the FBI be watching them?

The FBI was watching them, and had two agents in a van following the group's cross-country trek. The agents did not need to make an effort to conceal themselves since they were accompanied by five cars and vans full of reporters and camera crews. Each night of the journey people across America turned on their television sets to see and hear the latest on the cult fanatics who might explode at any minute. Millions watched in expectation of seeing a town destroyed in flames and screaming Remos manacled or lying in their own blood. Each evening the reporters carefully crafted their pieces to create and nurture that expectation.

The Remos included five women, six men, three children, two dogs, and three cats. They left Iowa in three rusted cars and a pickup loaded with furniture and household goods. On the fourth day of their journey they stopped at a campground in western South Dakota. As the sun set, Rev. Angle stood before the television cameras, his long beard lifting in the breeze, announcing that their journey was nearly over. Nearby stood Cremina Angle, the reverend's wife; Carl and Greta Clingmeier and their daughter Annie, an Iowa farm family that had lost their land, home, and machinery in the ever-worsening farm economy; Jeb and Letta Hudson and their two young boys, Charlie and Rank, from the coal fields of Kentucky; Li and Pinang Chew, recent South Korean immigrants; Charles "The Rock" and Selma Dinkins, unemployed, black factory workers and former tenant farmers from Alabama; and last, George Slow Bear, a Oglala Lakota, formerly from Wounded Knee, South Dakota, a recovering alcoholic.

Now they stood handling lizards and watching as their leader talked to the television cameras and reporters, looking like a Biblical prophet of old. "The Lord has stretched out His arm and pointed West," he said, turning and pointing to the sunset. "There lies our journey's end. Praise God!"

"Praise God!" the Remos chanted.

"Aber dongkleinstinkerfust mabbellines abdunktermein," Angle began in tongues, raising his hands as his people began murmuring and swaying, lifting and shaking their arms and uttering strange sounds that grew louder, forming an unearthly chorus on the darkening plain.

"Mimfippery glopsholap!" yelled Carl Clingmeier, and the other Remos shouted agreement as the cameras rolled and reporters grinned.

When they were again silent a reporter asked, "Do you know where you're headed?"

"Yes," Angle said.

"Where?"

"That's between the Lord and me."

"He won't mind if you tell me," the reporter said.

"Leave us," Angle said, and the reporters and camera and sound crew reluctantly returned to their vehicles.

When they were out of earshot, Angle told his people,"God has spoken to me, brothers and sisters, with a sign so unmistakable that it burns with an incandescent flame in the very cells of my brain!"

"Tell us the word, brother Angle," said Carl. "Say it!"

"Say it, Reverend!" said Mrs. Clingmeier. "Tell us the revelation!"

Reverend Angle opened the Grand Tally atlas and held it over his head. "God," said the reverend, "put this atlas into my hands this afternoon, at the gas station in Mandan."

"Amen," intoned his flock.

"As we drove today and I studied this book, looking for a sign that would reveal our final destination, that place where we shall be swept up in glory to the sound of harps and the singing of angels!"

The Remos chorused, "Amen!"

"Did you find that sign, reverend?"Carl asked.

"I did!" Angle shouted. "I saw the sign with a blinding flash of light! . . . Montana!"

"Praise be to God!" his people shouted. "Hallelujah!"

"Why?" Angle asked. "Because the U.S. map in this atlas does not contain the state of Montana!"

There followed a stunned silence.

"Observe, brothers and sisters!"

Angle opened the atlas. "It is not here! And the state is NOT included in any other part of the atlas! God told us to travel west, and now he has shown us that Montana will cease to exist! WHY? Because He will strike it with the power of a five-hundred megaton hydrogen explosion!! BLAM! Incineration! Rapture! Blinding eternal love that will sweep up His blessed saints into His bosom on the day of reckoning!!"

"Praise Jesus, Glory hallelujah!" the Remos shouted.

"Aber dongkleinstinkerfust mabbellines abdunktermeiraising," Angle shouted as he began speaking in tongues.

In their reports that evening the correspondents emphasized that the Remos' final destination was still a mystery, but one that promised soon to be revealed. In the meantime they urged residents of the region to remain vigilant. As one reporter said, "You never know, in this day, when violence and tragedy will strike. Questions about the Remos rage throughout the medical profession. Are they psychotic? Are they a potential threat? Only time will tell. And, in the meantime," the reporter intoned solemnly, "we can only pray that everyone remains alert to potential danger, including . . . the Remos."

The next morning the nation's most popular A.M. talk show interviewed three experts. One, a student of cults, said that Angle's followers were lost souls, losers in the American system who had delivered up their freedom and autonomy to the prophet. He said they were paranoid and delusional. Such people, the unfortunates unable to make a place for themselves at America's bountiful banquet, could easily flip into violent rage once the expected end failed to materialize. The second expert, a psychiatrist, agreed with everything the cult expert said, except that he assured listeners that Angle's problem was not a delusional paranoia but schizophrenia. The third expert, a Methodist minister who studied Evangelical groups, felt that it was entirely likely that the group would commit mass suicide, and that it was imperative the children be taken from their parents as soon as possible. He urged immediate action by appropriate federal agencies.

Hardwicke, who was watching from his bureau office, nodded grimly and switched off the set.

Then the perky little woman who co-hosted the morning show said, "Now we'll look at the country where the Remos camped last night and try to get an idea of where they might be headed. Let's take a look at the new Grand Tally map of the United States—published just yesterday!"

A large map was projected onto a giant monitor. The picture focused on the western states. In western South Dakota, near Rapid City, appeared a red star.

"Here," said the perky co-host, "is where the Remos camped last night, about twenty miles from the state line. It is very likely that the group will continue moving west, which will bring them into"—she looked at the map—"Idaho." There was a pause. "This doesn't look right." She turned to look off-camera. "Is Idaho next to South Dakota?"

"Apparently so," chuckled her co-host.

The camera switched to him. He was grinning and shaking his head. "We're a little rusty on U.S. geography, huh?"

"Guess so, but it does look odd. At any rate, Idaho residents better beware that this group is nearby and likely to settle somewhere within their state."

Two hours earlier, the Remos had crossed the Montana state line.

7.

After Buck left with Cap and Byron, Lorene took a quick shower so she would not miss the opening of her morning TV program, "Rex and Sally Lou." "Rex and Sally Lou" was a celebrity interview and gossip show, and when Lorene watched it she felt a part of the bigger world. Rex and Sally Lou were sophisticated New Yorkers who lived glamorous lives and were frequent subjects of the tabloid press. Sally Lou was a bubbly, effervescent brunette who often mugged on camera. Rex was punchy and aggressive with a fast New York put-down sense of humor. He reminded people of a little Yorkie terrier that, from behind the safety of a fence, bites and snarls at bigger dogs outside.

Two years ago, Sally Lou had been found to be part owner of a celebrity fat farm and drying-out tank that employed hundreds of Third World children for pennies a day. The *National Tattler* had discovered that many of these children had been sold by their parents in a desperate attempt to earn a few days' food. When the conditions were exposed, Sally Lou wept and cried before her TV audience for weeks on end, saying how she loved children and would never ever want to hurt even the tiniest hair on their teeny heads. Besides, she had a child of her own. She swore she knew nothing of the enslaved youngsters, that she had only been to the fat farm three times, and then at night for gala events when she had not seen any children at all.

Many thousands of people wrote and called in to say she was an evil, lying, self-centered idiot, and many thousands defended her saying that someone as sweet as Sally Lou could not have known anything about such goings on and would never have tolerated them if she had.

Sally Lou's response was to sell her share of the fat farm and begin making guest appearances at fund-raisers for disadvantaged children. A year after the exposure she won a prestigious national award for her charitable work, by which time the public had forgotten all about the exploitation.

But a year after she won the award, her husband, a famous hair designer, was caught in the act with a buxom young blond. When he denied having the affair, the *National Tattler* published revealing photos of the two. For weeks following, Sally Lou went on and on about how she and Dickie, her husband, were doing all sorts of ordinary and fabulous things together. They were such a pair, made for each other. By her own confession, made many times on the show, Dickie was a sex machine who never got enough. Apparently not, thought many people.

Despite all these goings on, Lorene still loved the show. Her favorite segment was the card drawing. Each day Rex and Sally Lou would dip into a big bin on stage and draw out a card with the name and address of some woman somewhere in the United States. They would telephone her, chit chat a while, then ask her a question. If the woman answered correctly, she would win a prize, usually something like a stereo cabinet or a table and chairs or a VCR. For the past five years, Lorene had sent a card in every week.

This morning, as she dried herself in front of the TV, Rex said, "Do you want to announce our next guest or shall I?"

"Either one, Rex. I don't want to make a big deal out of it. Can we just do the show?"

"My-y-y-y-y we're grumpy this morning. What is our problem, princess?"

"Dickie only gave it to me once."

"Ohhhhhhh. Tsk tsk tsk. What a shame. Well"—suddenly shouting—"I DIDN'T GET ANY! Judy had a head cold. I should be the one complaining. But no, it's you. You have to get it fifty times a day, apparently, or you're out of sorts. Well, just don't bring that attitude with you to work. PLEEEZZZ!"

Sally Lou hung her head and said quietly. "Sorry."

"Apology accepted. Now, do you want to introduce our next guest?"

Perking up she said, "I'd be delighted. She's Jovina Rates, an accountant with Grand Tally, the world's greatest mapmaker."

"They are the greatest, aren't they?"

"Absolutely."

"They've been the greatest for over 200 years."

"That long?"

"Yeah."

"Wow. I didn't know that."

"Now you do. Live and learn."

"Guess so."

"Good. Now would you introduce our guest?"

Sally Lou made an exasperated face.

Rex threw up his hands and yelled, "Would you just bring out the guest!"

"Don't shout."

"All right, all right."

Sally Lou smiled at the camera and then said, "Please welcome one of Grand Tally's top accountants, Jovina Rates!"

The band struck up a lively tune, the audience burst into applause, and Ms. Rates, attired in a prim two-piece suit, strolled out.

Rex and Sally Lou got off their stools and shook hands with her. "Welcome to the show," Rex said. "I understand you folks have just issued a brand new atlas, the first in fifteen years."

"That's right."

"What makes this such a special atlas?"

"First, as you know, Grand Tally's *World Atlas* has been world renowned ever since the first was issued, over one hundred years ago."

"Oh, yes," Rex said.

"Well, this one has updated everything. We have information on rainfall, snowfall, information on timber, mining, you name it."

"In other words," piped in Sally Lou, "it's a gold mine of information."

"Absolutely."

"Here's a copy of the atlas," Rex said, holding one up and flipping through it for the camera. "Doesn't it just look stunning?"

"And don't forget the U.S. map," added Sally Lou.

"I'm not forgetting the MAP!" snapped Rex.

"Well I just . . . wanted . . . to be . . . of . . . help!!! . . . . Sorry!"

"Okay," said Rex, pretending to be put out, "let's look at the map of the United States."

The camera panned to the back wall, showing a blow-up of Tally's U.S. map. This was the segment Lorene had been waiting for.

"What makes this atlas extra special is the fact that for the first time we've combined the world atlas with the U.S. atlas."

"Speaking of maps, Rex," said Sally Lou, "it's about time to pick some cards."

Rex turned to Ms. Rates. "Do you see what a clever segue we did from Grand Tally into the card drawing?"

"Oh, yes," Ms. Rates nodded.

Sally Lou said: "Just so the people at home will know, let's remind them that every Friday we look for four winners."

"And all of those winners come to New York to compete for a prize," Rex added. "What prize do we have this week?"

A picture of a pink Cadillac appeared on the screen. Lorene gasped and pulled the towel around her.

"Whaddaya say we saunter over to the bin, Miss Sally, and pluck out a few cards?"

"Sounds good to me, Rex."

"Anything would sound good to you," Rex scoffed, winking

at the camera.

Then Sally Lou mugged, pretending to be irritated. The audience roared. Lorene guffawed and slapped her thighs.

"Are we going to pick the card or not?" Rex asked.

"Of course we are."

"Why don't you do the honors."

"I'd be pleased." Looking off stage Sally Lou said, "A drum roll, please." Then she pretended to roll up a sleeve on her sleeveless dress and dipped her arm into the bin, stirred up the cards and pulled one out.

Lorene crossed her fingers and murmured, "Oh please, oh please!"

"This card is from . . . . Lorene Simpson of Moosehead, Montana."

"Montana!" Sally Lou called excitedly.

"Moosehead, Montana!" Rex repeated.

Lorene's eyes bugged. Then she jumped up and screamed, "Oh my! Oh, my!"

Rex picked up the phone and dialed. Just then Lorene's two dogs started growling, then leaped at each other. They were snapping and biting and Lorene had her towel off and was whacking them with it when the phone rang. She picked up the receiver while yelling, "Shut up! Get out! Get out!"

Everyone in the studio audience and in every home across America that was tuned to "Rex and Sally Lou" heard Lorene shouting incomprehensibly.

Rex was saying, "Hello, Lorene? Can you hear me?"

More muffled shouts. Then Lorene almost yelled, "Hello!"

"May I please speak with Lorene Simpson?" Rex asked.

"Speaking!" Lorene called loudly.

"You don't have to shout!"

"She's excited, Rex," Sally Lou told him.

"What was going on there? What were those strange noises?"

"I was shouting at my dawgs. They was fighting. And I'm standing here buck naked, I just got out of the shower."

"Naked?"

"Yes, I didn't want to miss a minute of your show. I watch every day."

"Well, that's wonderful," said Sally Lou.

"What's it like out there in Montana?" Rex asked.

"Oh, it's a gorgeous day!"

"Then how come you're inside?"

"I don't want to miss your show. I LOVE you guys!"

"Well, we love you, Lorene. What do you guys do out there for fun?"

"Oh, we do a little of this and a little of that. Mostly that."

"I see. Sounds exciting," Rex said and rolled his eyes.

"Well, at least we're not likely to get killed by some crazy person or run over by a taxi," Lorene laughed.

"Well, you don't know what you're missing. You haven't lived until you've had a near miss with one of our Pakistani drivers!!!"

Sally Lou was shaking her head vigorously in agreement. "It's true!"

"Are you ready for the question?"

"Oh, yes."

"Good luck, Lorene," said Sally Lou.

"Thank you."

"Pay attention now, Lorene. Actually, as you live in the West, this question should be a snap for you. Are you a fan of western movies?'

"Oh, yes."

"All right. Can you tell me the name of John Wayne's male co-star in Red River?"

Without hesitating a moment, Lorene said, "Montgomery Clift."

"That's RIGHT!" Rex shouted.

Sally Lou began clapping her hands.

"All right," Rex said, "let's move over the the map. Let's find out exactly where you live, Lorene. Where is Montana?" He began looking at the Western states. "I don't see it."

"Oh, Rex," Sally Lou said, "you shouldn'tve slept through school twelve years. I warned you."

"It's not here, stupid. Look for yourself."

Sally Lou looked. "I don't see it, either."

"Ms. Rates, I hate to tell you, but I think your map is a piece of shsh—!"

"Rex!" Sally Lou warned, "Don't say it!"

Ms. Rates had been in a state of shock ever since Rex had announced that the winner was from Montana. Ever since Mr. Mason and his team had decided to omit the individual map of Montana from the atlas, it had somehow been decided that it should be omitted from the continental map too. This had been done in a time of hysteria. No one seemed to be able to think properly. The general excuse used was that they had to be consistent; furthermore, no one would care whether the state was cut or not.

She heard Rex saying, "Ms. Ra-a-a-ates!! I'm talking to you!"

She looked up.

"What happened to Montana?"

They waited for her answer.

"Montana," she said with a boldness that surprised herself, "is not a state."

"Not a state!!!"

"It was a territory, back in the 1800s. Parts of it were later absorbed into Idaho and Wyoming."

"Oh," Rex said flatly. The answer had obviously deflated him.

"I didn't know that," said Sally Lou.

"Most people don't. Just like a lot of people think that New Mexico is a part of Mexico."

"Oh, wow," Rex said. "That is ignorant."

Lorene's voice was shouting over the speaker. "Montana is a state!!" She kept shouting it until Rex said, "Would you pipe down!"

There was a moment of silence before Lorene said very firmly, "Montana is a state!"

"Yeah, right, and I'm the King of Jerusalem. Why don't you go soak your head."

In a sweet, sing-song voice Sally Lou said, "We don't appreciate prank calls."

"This is not a prank call!"

"We could nail you with the FCC if we wanted to be nasty," Rex warned. "What you've done is called harassment. H-A-R-A-S-S—"

Lorene broke in. "You're the ones who're harassing people. You're a bunch of flippin' smart-alecks is what you are."

"Just cut her off," Rex groaned and the line was cut. "Can you believe that?" he asked.

Sally Lou wondered, "Do you think Lorene was confused or was she putting us on?"

Ms. Rates said, "You just can't tell today."

"No, you can't" Rex agreed. "We've got to cut now for commercial break. We'll be right back. Don't go away."

CHAPTER TWO

Louise "Lou" Amstatter sat in front of the television in her apartment in Manhattan's fashionable east seventies, drinking her morning coffee and watching the show she most loved to hate, "Rex and Sally Lou." As president of RAM, one of the country's most vocal feminist organizations, Lou despised the prissy and bubbly Sally Lou, whom she claimed was an enormous drag on the feminist cause.

Lou had grown up on a Wyoming ranch where she had learned to ride broncs, drink whiskey, and shoot a forty-five. Her great-grandparents had come to Montana in 1875, staked out a ranch the size of Rhode Island, and survived the attacks of Red Indians, blizzards, droughts, and the influx of homesteaders. Lou inherited her grandparents' sense of independence and tough-mindedness.

At age thirteen she developed a crush on a calf roper a few years her senior. During high school this crush developed into an infatuation which climaxed when she delivered her virginity to the calf roper on the flatbed of his pickup. It was a short, brutal experience that forever soured her on men.

Now as Lou listened to Rex berate this Lorene Whoever-she-was, her ire grew. What the hell was going on? Lou thought, as her mouth dropped open and she heard Ms. Rates claim Montana did not exist and listened to Lorene's astonished exclamations and Rex's threats. After Lorene was cut off, Lou heard that fraud, Ms. Rates, explain that Montana had only been a territory.

Lou immediately called the station and tried to get through to the show's producer. He was unavailable. Okay, she thought, he's on the set. She gave the operator a piece of her mind and decided to call back. By the time the show was over and she called again, the producer's lines were busy.

So mad she was almost shaking as she held the phone, Lou punched in the numbers for Grand Tally. Instead of a person, she got a recorded message saying, "You have reached the offices of Grand Tally. Our hours are from 8:30 A.M. to 5:00 o'clock P.M.." Lou's blood pressure began to rise. "If you are calling from a touch tone phone, please press one." She pressed one. The voice returned. "If you are calling our billing department, press one. For book orders, press two. For customer service, press three. For editorial, press four." Lou punched four. The voice returned, "If you know your party's extension, you may press it at any time during this message. To hear a directory of names, press one." She didn't know anyone there! She was getting angrier. How did these morons expect to do any business if no one could talk to them? She wanted to get to an operator. How could she do that? Maybe she hadn't heard the first sequence of options correctly. She hung the phone up and dialed again. The irritating, perky voice of the speaker came at her again. She forced herself to listen. No, "operator" was not an option. The message was over and she couldn't remember what numbers to push for what. "Godammit!!!!" she yelled into the receiver. "No wonder you fuckheads can't make a decent fucking atlas! Your fucking brains are shoved up your ASS!"

She dialed again, but by the time the voice came on, she was boiling with rage and slammed the phone down. She grabbed her purse and headed for the door.

2.

Cap, Byron, and Buck sat in the back of Sidewinder's Bar & Dancehall in downtown Moosehead, sipping their beer. Behind the bar a sign read:

TONIGHT
BUSTER BUTTS AND HIS EIGHTBALLS
8 P.M. - 2 A.M.
Admission: $10
Ladies Free

"Well, Cap," said Buck, "when do you reckon Alfred and them are showing up?"

"Soon."

At a pool table next to them an Indian and a tall, lanky cowboy were shooting eightball. The Indian was chalking his cue stick and studying the table.

"They're thirty minutes late," Buck said.

"I intend to chew their ass out," said Cap.

Byron, who was on his fourth beer, said, "I'd say kick his fuckin' ass out."

"Whose?" Cap asked.

"Alfred's."

Cap shook his head.

The Indian leaned forward. He was wearing a bright red shirt and Levi's and a wide brimmed hat. His clothes were scuffed with dirt and his shirt was ripped.

"You callin' everyone together, Cap?" asked Buck.

"You better believe it," Cap said.

"Then where the hell are they?" Byron wanted to know.

"I count on every one of those boys," said Cap. "They'll be here."

"I betcha Alfred's done got his sorry ass drunk."

"Byron, why are you so down on Alfred?"

"Not just Alfred, Cap, but the whole sad bunch. Where are they when they're needed? Here we got us the biggest screw job the government ever tried to pull on us, wiping out an entire state, and those boys can't get their sorry butts over here. They talk awful big when the sky's clear and sunshiney, but let the clouds roll in an' those boys is gone."

Buck said, "I agree with Cap. They'll be here."

"They're thirty minutes late," Byron objected.

The Indian made his shot; the cue ball clicked against the five ball.

"Look at the Indian, will you," Buck murmured to Cap.

Cap looked at the Indian and nodded. "I been seein' that fella around lately. He showed up about a month ago."

Just then they heard a clattering of boots at the front and turned to see about ten of their friends stomp in.

Cap's hand shot up and Alfred and the boys strode over.

"Cap," Alfred said, "we got us a shitload of trouble. Me an' the boys was on our way over here when we got word that Sonny Horton's gun collection got cleaned out."

Brice Harlow, one of the newcomers said, "Thirteen shotguns, 3 AK-47s, all his hand grenades, his grenade launcher, his bazooka. The whole shootin' match got cleaned out. Stolen."

"They took his dynamite too," said Alfred.

"And shotgun shells," said Tory Anderson.

Cap stood up fast.

"Who done it?" Buck asked.

"We don't know," said Alfred.

"I know who done it," Cap said between set teeth.

"When'd it happen?" Buck asked.

"Sonny says it had to've happened sometime today," Brice answered, "while he was out ridin' fence."

"Where's Sonny?" Buck wanted to know.

"He's comin'" Alfred said. "He wanted to lock his place up first an' set booby traps."

"I said I know who done it," Cap said, louder this time.

The men looked at him.

"So does Buck," Cap added

The men looked at Buck, who knotted up his brows, trying to think what Cap meant.

"Byron does too," Cap said.

The men looked at Byron.

Then, simultaneously, Byron and Buck's mouths opened as Cap lifted the atlas so everyone could see it.

"The gov'mint!" said Byron.

"Exactly," said Cap.

"Whaddaya mean, 'the gov'mint'?" a big man named Bouncer asked.

"Lookee here, boys," Cap said, and opened the atlas to the U.S. map. "Look what they done to Montana."

The men crowded round and looked.

"I don't see Montana," Bouncer said.

"Lookit them other states," said Alfred. "Lookit Wyoming an' Idaho. Lookit that!"

"Lookit the Dakotas," Brice Harlow said. "They're drawn twice as big as they should be."

"What the hell kind of map is this?" Tory wanted to know.

"This here shows what the gov'ment plans on doin' to Montana," Cap said.

"This sum kind of joke?" Bouncer asked.

"It ain't no joke," said Buck.

"This here map company found out the gov'ment's plans to eliminate Montana and got a jump on things by publishing them. Now think about it," Cap said, "who in Montana is standin' up for American freedoms? Who's standin' between our gov'ment and them makin' us slaves?"

"We are," the men chimed.

"Exactly. We're all that's keepin' the gov'ment from makin' everybody in this state a slave to the United Nations. They know that too. That's why they're takin' our guns."

"I'll be a vulture's dinner," Bouncer said. "So that's it."

"You bet yer last shotgun shell it is," Byron told him.

"Bouncer," Cap said, "you wait here for Sonny, then come with him to the main cache. We better make sure that's secure. We'll see you there."

Cap and the boys left in a hurry. Once they were out the door the Indian and the cowboy quit their pool game and followed them outside.

3.

As the Moosehead division of the Montana Militia headed out of town, the Remos entered. Five minutes before, parked on a low rise overlooking Moosehead, the Voice of God had quietly told Enoch Angle that this was where he would soon send His Blessed Son, where the reverend and his flock should find a house and wait until the End. Now the Remos drove through town, looking for a real estate office, followed by five cars and three vans of journalists. Behind the journalists and camera crews came the two FBI agents.

When Angle finally spotted a real estate office he pulled his truck over. Inside, he explained to the agent that he and his friends were looking to rent a five or six bedroom house. The agent said he had just what they were looking for and drove the Remos down Highway 25 to a foreclosed home on the edge of the road.

That same day Angle and his followers signed a lease and moved in. While most cleaned the house, sweeping and mopping floors, dusting walls, carrying their few pieces of furniture inside, Mrs. Clingmeier wrote a shopping list for her husband. Minutes later, Carl Clingmeier returned to Moosehead for food and supplies.

The press, meanwhile, camped just outside the Remos' drive, raised their transmission poles, set up cameras, tripods and telescopic lenses. When Carl drove out, he had to ask one of them, whose van was blocking the lane, to please move. The man took his time but finally did. No one bothered to follow Carl.

4.

As Carl pulled out of his drive, Lorene was yelling at her TV.

"You fourflushin' liars! You lousy New York smart-asses, you cheated me out of my pink Cadillac! I'm gonna get that Cadillac, don't think I won't! And I'll get you, both of you lousy sonsofbitches!"

Just then the phone rang.

Lorene picked it up fast. "Hello," she barked.

"Lorene, I just seen how they flimflammed you out of the Cadillac. I couldn't believe it! What is going on??!!!"

"Jeannie," Lorene said to her friend, "I do not know what is going on, but I damn sure intend to find out. I intend to sue those lousy you-know-whats. They cheated me!"

"They shore as heck did. Claimin' Montana ain't a state. Where do they get off? And where'd they get that stupid map?"

"They musta made it up just to cheat me out of my car. They musta picked my card in advance, then had someone draw that stupid map so's they could claim I was harassin' them."

"Lorene, if you want a lawyer, my nephew's a lawyer in New York."

"Is he. I *need* a lawyer."

"I think you need to go to New York and confront those crooks, right on national TV."

"Yer right! I'm gonna do it. You wanna come with me?"

"Hell, yeah, I'll go. When do we leave?"

"Lemme call over to Billings to see when we can get a flight outa here."

"One thing, Lorene. I'll go there on condition you sue them."

"Course I'm gonna sue them. They humiliated me in front of millions of people."

"Remember, I'm goin' to New York to give you moral support."

"I appreciate it."

"So when I stand by you on national TV and later on in court, and tell them how this news affected your heart and how you got so mad you nearly died, I expect that you'll remember me, if you know what I mean."

"Huh?"

"Look, hon, are you buyin' my plane ticket to New York?"

"You know I don't have the money."

"And do I have the money to fly to New York?"

"Not exactly."

"Right. And how long is it gonna take me to pay back that bill? After all, it could cost me seven hundred dollars."

"Yeah."

"If you win a big lawsuit, or any lawsuit, you'll throw somethin' my way, won't you?"

"Course I will. And I'll buy us steaks big enough to choke a horse."

"All right, I'm in," Jeannie said.

Lorene called a travel agent in Billings who told her they would have to fly from Billings to Minneapolis and then transfer to a plane to New York—two seats on a 6:30 P.M. flight from Billings and another two seats on a 9:03 P.M. flight to New York. Lorene booked them.

She called Jeannie back, told her to be at her place at 4:30 that afternoon and got the number of Jeannie's nephew in New York. Lon Jones was out of the office when Lorene called and would not be back for another hour. She left her number and a brief message and paced back and forth chain smoking cigarettes, seeing the faces of those two morons up there on stage and that superior woman from the map company. Which was it? Grand Tally. What a bunch they must be to get involved in this swindle. She'd name them in the suit too. She'd sue Rex, Sally Lou, Grand Tally, and the show's producer. Maybe the state of Montana would like to get involved since it'd just been told by those New York smart-alecks that it didn't exist.

After a while Lorene's nerves got to her and she made herself a ham sandwich and opened a can of baked beans and spooned them out on a plate. She picked at her food while she imagined punching Rex right in his squirrelly little face and knocking him flat on the stage and running after that skinny little Sally Lou with her little tiny behind, coming up behind her and pushing her over, jumping on her and wringing her neck. She heard Sally Lou pleading, "No, no, no. Pleeaaasse," and weeping, saying, "I'm sorry for calling you names, I really am. Please forgive me.'"

Then she wondered where Buck and Cap and Byron had gone to. What the heck did they intend to do about Sheriff Brandt anyway? She wondered if they'd finally fix his behind. She had no more use for him than they did, or for the state legislature or the feds in Washington. They were all a bunch of crooks bought off by guys with money. But Lew Mitchell was a jerk and deserved to go to jail for a thousand things he had done that last year. If Lew Mitchell shot at somebody, let him get whatever he deserved, whatever maximum the law allowed. It sure as hell wasn't worth risking trouble for someone as no-account as Lew Mitchell.

An hour later Lon Jones called back and Lorene explained what had happened.

"Are you serious, Mrs. Simpson?"

"I'm as serious as a heart attack."

"But that was on national TV. How could they try to swindle someone on national TV? It'd be too obvious. They'd get caught right away."

"But they did it. Just get a copy of the show and see. I'll see you in New York tomorrow."

5.

The Travers were still driving on Highway 25, heading doggedly west. Mrs. Travers now had her arms crossed, for as far as they could see in all directions, the land rolled slightly under a big domed sky. No towns, no houses, no people.

"I'm safe with you behind the wheel, that's for sure."

Mr. Travers said nothing, just looked ahead. What was she referring to now? he wondered.

"When was the last time you checked the gas needle?"

Mr. Travers lowered his eyes. The needle was on empty.

"Empty," she said, then added quietly, "I'm so mad."

"Will you lay off?" said Mr. Travers.

"Lay off? Yeah, I'll lay off. I'll lay off now that we're stuck out in the middle of the desert with no water, no traffic, no houses, nothing. A desert! We're stuck in a desert with no gas. We don't have any food, we don't have any water, we don't have a telephone. I'm in good hands with Charlie," she added sarcastically.

Mr. Travers couldn't count the number of times she had used that line. "All right," he said, "I made a mistake. All right? I made a mistake."

"This is not the same as letting the garbage rot in the kitchen so the whole house stinks or not cleaning the toilet bowl after you've peed on the sides. Do you understand that this is more serious? Do you!?" She glared at him.

He looked at her a moment, then glanced away.

"We could die out here."

"I hardly think so."

"What do you know about it? When was the last time you took a survival course, huh? Oh yeah, trust Charlie Travers to get us out of this one. What are your plans?"

"We haven't run out of gas yet."

"We'll run out in a minute!" She looked out her side of the car. "Oh, sometimes I could kill you."

Mr. Travers ignored her as best he could and concentrated on the road ahead, hoping to see a car or truck. There hadn't been many vehicles this morning, but he was not afraid. He knew that one would come along eventually, but to get as much mileage as possible he kept his foot evenly on the gas pedal and ran the car at fifty-five. Soon it began sputtering, then died. Mr. Travers coasted the car to a stop on the side of the road. Mrs. Travers wouldn't look at him.

Ten minutes later they saw a smudge of dark on the road at the horizon line. Slowly, the smudge grew larger, then transformed itself into a car. Mr. Travers was standing alongside his car when the other vehicle pulled up and Carl Clingmeier rolled down his window and asked, "Need a lift?"

"We ran out of gas," said Mr. Travers. "Do you have some to sell?"

"Nope. And I don't have a tube to siphon with either."

"How far's the nearest town?"

"Twenty miles that way," Carl answered, pointing back the way he'd come. "Moosehead. I just come from there. Tell ya what. If ya want to ride with me to my place, we'll get ya some gas."

The Travers hesitated.

"I'll drive you back," said Carl.

"Okay," said Mr. Travers and began walking over to the stranger's car. Mrs. Travers did not want to get out. She did not want to accept a ride from a stranger but was even more reluctantto stay alone in the car. Still she got out and called after her husband, "Are you just going to leave the car?"

Mr. Travers turned around. "What do you mean?"

"We need to lock it," she said in an exasperated tone.

"Well, then, lock it," he said.

"The automatic lock is broken, remember?"

He walked back, angry with her for having caught him. Mrs. Travers got out and Mr. Travers locked the car and looked at her.

"Is that all?" she asked.

"What!?" he demanded with growing irritation.

"We need to leave a note. Here, I have a pencil."

Mr. Travers rummaged in his pockets and found a scrap of paper in his wallet.

"That's too small," she said.

"It will have to do," he said and wrote out, "Ran out of gas. Be back soon."

Mr. and Mrs. Travers got in the stranger's car.

"Where you headed?" Carl asked.

"My brother's house," Mrs. Travers answered, "somewhere in this Godforsaken country."

"You don't like it here?" Carl asked as his shoulders twitched and he stepped on the pedal.

"No," said Mrs. Travers.

"I think it's great!" Carl said.

Mrs. Travers grunted.

"Do you ranch?" Mr. Travers asked.

"Friends and I do odd jobs." Carl's mouth twitched, then his head shook spasmodically. "We're gonna raise chickens and grow a big"—twitch— "vegetable garden."

"Where you from?" Mr. Travers asked.

"Ioway."

"How did you come to this place?" Mrs. Travers inquired.

"The Lord brought us. He said, 'Flee the heathen and seek ye my blessing,'"—twitch—"and led us here. There's a lot of sinnin' where we come from."

"There's a lot of crooks and sick people all over," Mrs. Travers agreed.

"Are you folks Christian?" Carl asked with a jerk of his head.

"We're Methodist," said Mr. Travers. "We think we're Christian." He gave his wife a glance.

Carl said, "There's a lot of folks think they're Christian that're headin' straight for hell fire at the speed of light. The Day of Judgment is comin' soon. Real soon. July thirty-first, this year. And a lot o' people'll be caught with their pants down. Garblastud el malomud dishistickel!!! InFIERMONT GAZONTEZZ!!!!!"

Mr. and Mrs. Travers looked at the stranger, then at each other. Both thought they had made a terrible blunder in accepting this ride. Mr. Travers was sure this man with a twitch had a gun. He wished he had brought one of his own handguns with him. Damn! Why hadn't he? He began sweating.

"Praise Jesus!" Carl shouted. "Praise Him forever and ever." He shook his head quickly back and forth and pounded the steering wheel. The car swerved from side to side. "Boy! I get worked up when I think about Jesus and the salvation he offers a rotten sinner like me." He looked up and closed his eyes. "Thank you JEsus!"

Mrs. Travers wanted to tell him to watch the road.

"Jesus wanted you to run out of gas so you'd meet me. It was God's will!" he shouted and shivered all over.

Mrs. Travers watched him, digging her nails into her palms. If this maniac struck, Charles would be no help. This crazy would clobber Charles on the head and drag her outside the car to some bushes and have his will of her and cut her throat. She began chewing her lip.

"God works in mysterious ways," Carl said, looking at them, the sweat popping off his brow and neck.

"Yeah, He does," Mr. Travers quietly agreed.

"You see, you folks are Methodist, but have you really accepted Jesus!? Really accepted Him?" He slammed a palm on the dashboard; his voice grew louder. "Are you praying with all your hearts for His love and presence in your lives? Are you waiting to be swept up into eternal glory when He comes again in the Fires of Wrath? Are you?"

Both Traverses saw Carl's strange expression, saw the sweat rolling down his face, the cords on his neck bulging, his eyes popped wide, his hair disheveled. Both knew the answer he expected.

"Oh, yes," said Mr. Travers. "We are waiting for Jesus. Yes. Definitely."

Carl raised his head as it shook spasmodically. Both arms flew off the steering wheel as he shouted, "Amen, brother and sister. AMEN!!! Praise Jesus! I knew there was a reason God let you run out of gas."

Mr. Travers sat with open mouth. In the back seat, Mrs. Travers began to pee.

"Welcome to Rosebud County," Carl said, looking at them and nodding his head. "My name is Carl Clingmeier. And we're gonna be friends. Lemme tell ya, your days of searching and wondering are over."

6.

That afternoon FBI agent Chip Kline, one of the two agents following the Remos, called Washington to say that the subjects had rented a house and outbuildings near Moosehead, Montana.

Hardwicke's reaction was, "Keep watchin' em. See if you can get a wire into that house."

"Yes, boss," Kline said, "as soon as I can." He told Hardwicke about the reporters camped outside the house.

"Get 'em out of there," Hardwicke said.

Kline and his cohort, Siggy Harris, got out of their car and went over to the knot of journalists.

"Mr. Kline," asked Gus Harvey, the well-known New York CDC network reporter, "can you tell us what the bureau's plans are?"

"The bureau's plan is to get you away from this property. Three hundred yards away."

"Three hundred?" another journalist said. "We can't cover anything at that distance."

"You're obstructing our work."

"Can you tell us what your plans are?"

"I told you. Three hundred yards away."

"This is county property," countered Harvey.

"How'd you like county jail for obstruction of justice?" Kline snapped. "If any of you come back here, anytime, I'll pick you up. Promise."

The reporters got the point, climbed in their cars and vans and drove off. Eyes from inside the house watched the proceedings. When the others left, Kline and Harris returned to their car.

"The Man wants us to bug that house and I got an idea," Kline said, and he and Harris drove to Moosehead where Kline bought workclothes, a toolbox, and tools, then rented a van and drove back to the house. When they got within sight of the house, Harris got out and Kline continued on alone. Wearing the workclothes and carrying the toolbox, he knocked on the front door.

This was not easy for Kline. It was his first field assignment and the Remos seemed unstable. You never knew when one of these groups would go ballistic. There had been ten standoffs with cults and militia-types in the last year alone. Agents were getting promoted like crazy. Journalists were writing books on the standoffs and everyone was appearing on TV talk shows. FBI and ATF sharpshooters were writing manuals on how to pick off a suspect at a hundred yards. These Remos were clearly wackos and a threat to Montana peace, probably a threat to each other. He had to arrest them, kill them if necessary. There would be no TV cameras or home videos or reporters around when the time came to do it. And in his reports he would use words like "neutralize" and "take out." He had been practicing his fast draw for one hour each day since he'd gotten this assignment, thirty minutes after morning coffee and thirty after dinner.

The problem with America was that everyone was suspect. Everyone was a potential threat to domestic security. You never knew who would go off or when. He had seen it on the dozen TV talk shows which every day featured trash of all colors who were sleeping with their sister's or brother's betrothed, even with their brothers or sisters, with their in-laws, mothers, fathers, you name it. Many of these had also betrayed close relatives, double-crossed employers or employees, had stolen, lied, cheated, broken every one of the ten commandments and bragged about it. Lots of them and millions of others were drug addicts or alcoholics, and violent. They robbed at gunpoint and cleaned out bank accounts with the stroke of a keyboard.

They were shooting people on the streets and sending letter bombs through the mail. Scores of them, he knew through FBI intelligence, were suspected of making nerve gas and biological weapons or storing ingredients for bombs. The problem was, you stamped out one potential disaster and ten more sprang up. Now he was trying to stamp out one that had the capacity to wipe out a hundred or more innocent bystanders.

One of the Remos' children, Annie Clingmeier, carrying a ginkgo lizard on her shoulder, answered Kline's knock.

"Hello," Kline said. "Is your mommy or daddy here?"

The little girl turned and called, "Mommy, there's a man here."

A woman about twenty-seven came to the door, pushing back strands of hair from her face. "Yes, can I help you?"

"Ma'am," said agent Kline, "I'm Justin Parker from the Rosebud County Inspection Office. Unlike most counties in most states we require electrical inspections of all houses. May I come in?"

"I never heard of this."

"It's unusual. We do it for your own safety. If I find any substandard or dangerous wiring, I make note of it. You then have thirty days to fix the problem."

"I never heard of nothin' like this."

At this moment another woman, Letta Hudson, came to the door. Kline's palms began to sweat. He nodded hello to her and said to Mrs. Clingmeier, "I know, ma'am. But it's for your own good."

"Come back here this afternoon, would you?"

Just then the Chews, Jeb Hudson, the Dinkinses, the Angles, and George Slow Bear were in the back yard, spading up a patch of ground for a garden. Greta Clingmeier didn't want this man in the house alone with her and Letta and the kids.

"I can't come back, ma'm. I've got to be fifty miles down the road in eighty minutes. That doesn't leave me much time."

"Make it another day."

"I'm booked for the next two weeks and you're required by law to have this house inspected no later than the tenth day after occupancy. If it's not done by then you will have a substantial fine."

Kline could see the suspicion on Mrs. Clingmeier's face fade away.

"Well . . ." she hesitated and turned to the other woman. "What do you think, Letta?"

"We don't want a fine."

"Okay," Mrs. Clingmeier said, opening the door, "come on in."

As he stepped inside, Kline noticed two boys in the kitchen off to his right. He thought he would start his "inspection" there.

"Watch out you don't step on the lizards," Annie said. Kline looked down and saw about a dozen lizards scurry to safety under the ratty chairs and sofa. He shivered, then looked at the women.

"You aren't afraid of lizards, are you?" Letta asked.

"Yeah, guess I am."

"Nothin' to be afraid of. They're God's creatures too."

"Yeah," Kline said, and wondered why this cult liked them. "Are they pets?"

"They're servants of the Lord, same as us," Letta said.

"Letta," said Mrs. Clingmeier, "this man has business to do. He's in a hurry. He's gotta be fifty miles down the road in eighty minutes. Ain't that right?"

"Yes, ma'am, it is."

"Well," Mrs. Clingmeier said, "you can start your inspection any time."

As Kline pretended to check the wiring, flipping light switches on and off, he noticed that the three children were watching him. "Aren't you youngsters supposed to be in school?" he asked, wondering if one of them might try to hack him with a kitchen knife when his back was turned. They looked inbred and dirty enough to do it.

"We are in school," a little boy said.

"We home school them," Letta said. "We don't want them mixin' with people who'll put junk in their haids."

Jeez, Kline thought, junk in their heads. You need your brains washed under the sink.

"Letta," said Mrs. Clingmeier, "why don't you get the children back to their studies. They've finished eating. I'll clean up dishes later."

"Okay. Children, you heard. Let's go back to the living room."

While Letta and Mrs. Clingmeier and the children had been talking, Kline had succeeded in planting a bug behind the toaster. Now, as Letta and the children trooped back into the living room, Kline, accompanied by Mrs. Clingmeier, pretended to check the wiring in other rooms. Even under her watchful eye, he was able to plant bugs in two other rooms, all the while ready to drop her with a slug if she made any sudden move. At the end he said, "You're in good shape. You meet inspection, congratulations." As he drove off, Mrs.Clingmeier watched him from the door, feeling that something was not right.

7.

Carl Clingmeier drove his car fast down the slope to the Remos' newly rented house at the bottom of the hollow.

Olivia Travers, sitting in the back seat and afraid of the speed and the sight of a lone house, clung tightly to the door handle.

Mr. Travers's heart pounded wildly but he managed to say, "I thought you were goin' to get us to a station."

Carl said, "No, I said I'd getcha gas here. Besides, I wanted ya to meet the folks. They're Christians too!"

He braked the car to a sudden stop and it slid sideways on the gravel.

Mr. Travers was suddenly aware of the sweat on his palms and the dryness of his mouth. This man Clingmeier was a crazed drug addict who was going to kill him and Olivia. For years he had read and heard and thought about stranded motorists victimized and murdered by psychotic passersby! How ironic! Now he and Olivia were the targets!

Carl jumped out and called loudly, "Last stop! Everybody out!"

Mr. and Mrs. Travers knew what that meant and did not move. Mrs. Travers couldn't think and Mr. Travers didn't know whether to die in the car or take his chances outside, possibly in some horrible place, maybe a filthy outhouse.

A little girl came to the door and opened it. She saw her daddy looking at the car and at two people in it. "Who're they?" she asked.

Mr. Travers could only vaguely see a figure at the door. Mrs. Travers was too frightened to see anything, but somehow—mechanically, unintentionally—she opened her door.

Carl turned to his daughter. "They're poor Christians who ran out of gas, Annie."

The girl stepped outside. She was covered with lizards clinging to every bit of her clothes and to the top of her head.

Mr. Travers gasped at the sight.

"What's the matter with them?" Annie asked.

Carl turned and looked at the two rigid bodies in his car. "What's the matter?" he asked.

"Nothing," Mr. Travers stammered.

"Don't you want to get out and stretch?"

"No, we're okay."

"Ma'am?" Carl asked. "You look scared to death. What's the matter?"

Looking at Annie, Mrs. Travers began to choke. "Ah ah ah aggle thug thg tha—"

Carl popped his neck forward, straining for a closer look

at Olivia. Looking up and gasping for air she saw the sudden move, drew a deep breath and went: "Nnnuhnnuh nah nah nah uunhhh!" and began hyperventilating.

Carl stretched up, his hands raised in the air, threw his head back and shouted, "Glory hallelujah amen praise Jesus merciful God she speaks in tongues benigthet thisis thanglosome LOBBERnasthy thingumbajebub namerath homerusonmoron thosugalal THANG LAH!!!!!"

Mrs. Travers fell sideways out of the car.

CHAPTER THREE

Lou Amstatter hailed a cab one block from her apartment and headed downtown for Grand Tally's offices. Lou lived on East Seventy-Third Street and Grand Tally's offices were on West Fifty-Third, and what might have been a forty minute walk turned into a one-hour cab ride.

The cabby spoke two or three words of English and had but a fleeting acquaintance with New York City street names and numbers. He swung his cab east when he should have turned west, he got caught in a traffic jam, and after Lou started yelling at him, he swerved to pass a truck and succeeded in forcing a bicycle messenger into a parked car. The messenger lay stunned on the pavement. Lou flung open the door, ignoring the cabby's incoherent cries for his fare and the unconscious messenger, and headed south for Grand Tally offices. The delay had done her temper no good.

It was noon when she arrived at the seventy-five story building where she was immediately confronted by a desk with two uniformed men seated behind it. Without breaking stride she sized up the situation. If she stopped at the desk and told them her name and business, she would most likely be denied permission to enter. She knew no one at Grand Tally, though possibly someone there had heard of her. Her message would no doubt be delivered to some flunky.

"May I help you?" one of the guards inquired.

"Yes, I'd like to speak to an editor at Grand Tally."

"Do you have an appointment?"

"No."

"I can't let you up then. Would you like to leave a message?"

"I want to speak with someone."

"What about?"

"The atlas."

"Your name, please?"

"Louise Amstatter."

The man began dialing his phone.

Lou realized that at best they would send down an assistant to a sub-editor's assistant, some twenty year old who could care less about anything. She turned and walked back outside. How could she have been so stupid as to have come down there? She hailed another cab and gave the driver the address of the *New York Times* building on West Forty-Second, a five block ride, then realized she had better go to the *Times* armed with proof. But the nearest bookstore was blocks away. She gave the driver her new destination. There she thumbed through the Grand Tally atlas and, sure enough, the state of Montana was omitted from the collection of state maps and, even more outrageously, from the continental map. The surrounding states of Wyoming, Idaho, and North and South Dakota had all been grotesquely distorted to fill the space of the missing state. Just like the continental map on that mindless television show. Her anger flared as she looked at this incredible invention and wondered how Grand Tally could be so stupid as to omit Montana. She wouldn't bother confronting anyione there; they obviously could care less about what they had done. She dragged her cell phone out of her purse and called *Times* reporter Rita Brockman who had written favorably about her in several articles. Everyone at the *Times* knew of Lou Amstatter.

"Unbelievable," was Brockman's reaction a half hour later as she looked at the evidence.

"Get a clip of the show," Lou suggested.

"Oh, I will," said Brockman. "Thanks for the lead."

2.

The Moosehead contingent of the Montana Militia were huddled together under the cottonwood trees as Sonny Horton came roaring up in a pickup truck and skidded to a stop.

Ten voices began clamoring at once. "See anything? See any tire tracks? Find anything at your place that could lead us to the thieves?"

"One lead," said Sonny. "This." He held up a piece of red cloth.

"What is it?" Buck asked.

"I think it's off a woman's dress," Sonny said.

"You found it in your arms cache?" Cap asked.

"Shore did, Cap."

"Well, I'll tell ya," said Cap, "whatever government bastard stole that cache has got their eye on this cache here. You can bet."

"How do we know that?"

"Whoever done it is followin' us. They probably got their eyes on us right now. And maybe, just maybe, it was an inside job."

"You mean one of us done it? One of us is a government agent?"

"Exactly."

"Wheeeewww!!!"

"Whoa!"

"Don't that beat all!"

The men suddenly looked at one another suspiciously with brows furrowed, noses squinched, eyes squinty.

"Which one?"

"Maybe it ain't just one."

"Oh Lord, how we gonna ketch the traitor?"

"We'll ketch 'im."

"When we do I'll put a bullet in his haid."

"I'll cut the sonuvabitch's throat."

"I'll make 'im a girl."

More looking, squinching, squinting.

Then: “Cap!!! How we gonna sniff this traitor out?”

That was Byron. Everyone looked at him, then at Cap.

“First off, we’re gonna load everything here into my pickup an’ Sonny’s pickup. Then Sonny an’ me are gonna drive off an hide it sumwhere. I figure Sonny’s the only one here I can be sure about.”

“Oh, yeah?” asked Buck, “how come?”

“Cause Sonny ain’t got the brains to think of stealin’ his own arms cache and blamin’ it on someone else.”

“But what if it wasn’t an inside job?” Tory Anderson asked.

“We’re gonna investigate,” Cap announced. “What we do know is that the thief, or one of the thieves, was wearin’ somethin’ red. All right, let’s get the pickups loaded.”

The men started to move towards the arms cache.

“Hold on, Cap,” Byron said. “What about Lew Mitchell? Ain’t we gonna spring him?”

“We’ll spring Lew and take care of Sheriff Brandt, but first we’re gonna take care of these weapons.”

3.

“You’re telling me you know more than Grand Tally!?” Bruce Jelton, Rex and Sally Lou’s producer, was on the phone with an irate viewer. “Montana no longer exists! Get it through your stupid head!” He slammed down the phone.

“Eddie!” he called to an intern across the room. “I want you to make a tape to handle all these fucking calls we’re getting.”

“What do you want me to say?”

“‘If you’re calling to complain about today’s show because you think Montana is a state, stick your fucking head up your goddamn ass.’”

“You serious?”

“If you can’t handle this Eddie, I’ll get another intern this morning. I got a list of names ten feet long. Now . . . . . . do you think you can make a tape for me?”

“Yes, Mr. Jelton.”

As Eddie trotted out of the room, Jelton muttered, “Dickhead."

He had turned back to his desk and was jotting notes when Rex came into the room. "Jelton! What's this crap about Montana? Does it or does it not exist?"

"Do you give a shit?"

"It's my fucking credibility! My reputation!"

"What credibility? You're an entertainer!"

"I don't want to look like a jerk!"

"I got news for you. As far as half the population in this country is concerned, you're the biggest joke in the industry. Do you know how many letters we get each week telling us to yank you from the show?"

"It can't be too many cause I'm still on! So don't get smart with me! Just remember your contract is with me and Sally Lou. If we want you out, you're gone!"

"You want to fire me now? Go ahead. Fire me. Then who's going to cover your ass?"

"Just don't get so smart!"

"But I am! That's why you hired me."

Sally Lou rushed into the room. "One of the camera crew says he grew up in Wyoming, thirty miles south of Montana! That state actually exists!"

"The mapmaker said it didn't," Jelton replied. "They're the authorities, not you."

"But I think I have fans out there!" Sally Lou whined.

"If it is a state, how many people do you think live out there? A hundred? Two hundred? Give me a break." He turned back to his notes.

"What are you doing at a time like this, Jelton?" Rex barked.

"Look," Jelton said, "just let me handle this, okay?"

"I don't care if there's only a hundred people in Montana," Sally Lou whined, "they're sweet lovely people who tune in every morning to see me while they have their morning coffee. They count on me."

Jelton held his brow in his hands. "You are so stupid it is fucking unbelievable. Who wipes your ass for you?"

"I do it myself."

"I don't believe it."

"Jelton!" screamed Rex. "Get a fucking intern to go to a fucking library and look at a map of the country."

"I hire interns to do more important stuff than that. You just SAW a fucking map or are you so dense you've already forgotten?"

"I think that map's a piece of shit!"

"What do you know about it? You ever been to Montana? . . . . Huh? Of course not."

"Jelton, this fucking show is on the line!"

"The show is not on the line! We didn't make a mistake. We didn't make the map. Grand Tally did. And why the hell do you think they would omit a state if it existed?"

"Maybe someone screwed up."

"That big a screwup? They've got proofreaders and fact checkers, they've got a two hundred year plus history! Can you hear me Rex baby? Over two hundred years!!!!

"Maybe you're right."

"What about the cameraman?" Sally Lou pleaded.

"The guy's a cameraman, right? How smart can he be? If the guy could count to two he'd have himself a decent job. He probably heard some story about the days when Montana was a territory and he got it mixed up in his head. Who are you going to believe, him or Grand Tally?"

Rex exhaled and his shoulders dropped. "Yeah, you're probably right."

"You think so?" Sally Lou asked.

"Yes!!!" Jelton said. "Just go out have yourself some roast duck and a bottle of Chateau Lafite for lunch and you'll forget about it, I guarantee. By tomorrow that prank call will've been forgotten."

"Yeah," said Rex, "you're probably right."

"I hope so," said Sally Lou.

"I am right."

"You up for lunch?" Rex asked Sally Lou.

"Yes, yes, yes. I could use a drink."

4.

When Mrs. Travers fell out of the car, Carl screamed, "Praise Jesus! Lord, touch all of us as you have touched this woman! Fill us with your Holy Spirit!"

Mr. Travers jumped out of the car and knelt by his wife.

The screen door opened and Mrs. Clingmeier stepped out.

Mr. Travers turned to them, pleading, "Don't kill us! Don't kill us!"

Carl, meanwhile, was walking in circles and praising the Lord. Annie, with lizards clinging to her, walked to the car and stared at Mrs. Travers. A lizard dropped from the girl's shoulder and scuttled towards Mr. Travers. He screamed. Mrs. Clingmeier ran over, yelling, "What happened?"

At this noise, Letta Huson stepped outside. She saw Carl, still talking to God, and walked to the far side of the car where Mrs. Travers was lying on the ground.

"The Lord has touched her!" Carl yelled.

"Amen!" Letta shouted.

"Praise Jesus!" Carl called.

"Praise Him, aMEN!" Letta shouted again.

"Bless you, Lord, for entering this woman's life!" Carl shouted, hopping up and down.

"Amen!" Letta added, throwing her arms skyward. "Jesus, I get more excited by you every day! There's no end to your miracles! No end to what you can accomplish! Amen!"

The two of them were yelling, "Praise Jesus!" as Mr. Travers began crying.

Mrs. Clingmeier stood over Mrs. Travers and announced in loud tones: "This woman's not touched by God, she's swallowed the Devil! She's drunk!"

"No, darlin'," said her husband, "she has been touched by the Holy Spirit!"

"My foot, she has! She can't stand on her feet! Lady," she announced, addressing the unconscious Mrs. Travers, "You are a disgrace to womankind! Have you no self-respect? Where is your pride? Do you know what God has planned for the likes of you? Hell fire! Eternal damnation! Oh, yes, don't look at me that way, lady! I've read my Bible. I know God's Word. I know what He intends for the likes of you, dead drunk at one in the afternoon!!!"

"She feels God's spirit," Mr. Clingmeier insisted.

"Hallelujah!" Letta shouted.

"Spawn of the Devil!" yelled Mrs. Clingmeier.

At this point Mrs. Harris trotted outside, saw the fallen woman and knelt beside her, put an ear to Mrs. Travers' mouth and listened. "She's breathing," she said. "Let's get her inside."

Hearing the shouting and screaming, Chip Kline and Siggy Harris had run from the trees by the side of the road, down the incline towards the front of the house. At the same moment the Remos, who had been working in the back, came running around front. Kline saw a man kneeling on the ground and heard him pleading, "Don't kill me! Don't kill me!"

Then he saw the men lift the fallen woman while others grabbed the kneeling man, forcing him up, and heard him sob as they dragged him into the house behind the woman. Kline and Harris drew their guns and were running towards the group shouting, "FBI! You're under arrest!" when Kline tripped and fell. Harris, running behind him, fell over Kline and both guns went off.

At the sound of the yelling the press hopped in their cars and sped to the Remos' drive where they jumped out with cameras rolling. They arrived in time to tape the Remos in a huddled mass outside the house with Kline on the ground and Harris standing, holding his gun and taking aim. They heard Harris yell and saw the group pushing to get through the open door, carrying a woman with them. Then they heard the agent's gun go off once more and saw splinters fly off the side of the house and more people squeeze inside, dragging the unconscious woman with them.

And then the agent lying on the ground, Kline, was yelling and the standing agent, Harris, was reloading his gun. Then Harris began dragging his partner back towards the trees.

"Dynamite! Dynamite!" Gus Harvey whispered excitedly,

directing his cameraman to get a close-up of the agents. "This is Pulitzer stuff!" he crowed. As the agents disappeared behind the trees he said, "Now get the house. Close-up on the windows."

5.

Rex and Sally Lou sat at Rex's table at his favorite midtown restaurant, Le Filet Mignon, New York's finest steak house. Rex was carving into a nicely marbled ten-ounce filet with a side of asparagus and a baked potato with sour cream and chives. He had a five leaf lettuce salad lightly covered with balsamic vinegar and extra virgin olive oil. To top it off he had ordered his favorite ale.

Sally Lou, on the other hand, was feeling much too fluttery to eat anything besides a Caesar salad.

"You're taking this whole thing too seriously, kid," Rex told her. "Take doctor Rex's advice, have a big steak, a bottle of wine, and take the rest of the day off."

"First off, I never eat anything as heavy as steak," Sally Lou said. "It doesn't sit in my stomach. You know that. Second, as much as I would like to drink a whole bottle of wine, I can't take the day off. Ruthie is having a piano recital at school this afternoon. I want to be there." She flashed Rex a smile and took a deep drink from her glass of Chardonay.

Ruthie was Sally Lou's daughter, and, according to Sally Lou's daily reports to television audiences, Ruthie was surely the most brilliantl and talented child in the country.

"Good," Rex said as he forked a hunk of steak into his mouth.

Just then a gentleman with a linen jacket and bow tie came up to their table and put a hand on the back of Sally Lou's chair and leaned towards Rex. "So Montana's not a state."

"Oh, Wellstone, go soak your head," Rex snapped. "I'm trying to eat."

"Hi, Dickie," said Sally Lou.

"Hello, precious. I saw you two this morning. What the hell was that about?"

"Well, if you saw it," Rex responded, "then you know what it was about."

"Not really. Was that a put-on?"

"That screeching woman on the telephone?" Rex asked.

"No, this business about Montana not being a state."

"No, it's not," said Sally Lou. "That was not a put-on. You saw that woman from Grand Tally. She said it wasn't a state. Didn't you see their map?"

"I thought," Dickie said, "that perhaps your producer had it made up."

"I'm not in the joking mood, Dickie," said Rex.

"Listen, I'm having an impromptu party for Marilyn tonight about six-thirty," Dickie said. "A light dinner. Both of you, come if you can and bring your spouses."

"Oh, I'd love to Dickie," said Sally Lou. "I'll see what's on the schedule."

"I think I can," said Rex. "I think Judy and I are both free."

"It's informal," Dickie said. "Bye the way, I don't know where you two went to school, but Montana is a state. Be prepared for a major ratings drop. Bye-bye."

As Dickie walked away, Sally Lou lifted her glass with an unsteady hand, took another deep drink, then said, "Excuse me, I have to go to the rest room." Within a minute, Sally Lou's fifteen dollar glass of Chardonay and her Caesar salad were spiraling down a bowl in the women's room.

6.

Immediately after Lou Amstatter left the *Times*' offices, Rita Brockman put her current story on hold and called Grand Tally. The message machine offered five numbered options, but Brockman ignored them and pushed O for "operator." She identified herself to the woman on the phone and said she would like to speak to Leslie Driggs.

"Just a moment, please."

She waited.

Another voice came on. "Mr. Driggs' office, may I help

you?"

"Yes. This is Rita Brockman from the *New York Times*. I'd like to speak with Mr. Driggs about your new atlas."

"I'll connect you with corporate communications. Just a moment please."

Before Brockman could object, she was put on hold. Another voice wanted to know how she could be of assistance. Rita identified herself and said she wanted to speak to someone regarding the new atlas.

"Certainly," the voice said. "I'll see if Jonathan Ryder is available."

Jonathan Ryder was one of the office underlings. He picked up the phone. "Jonathan Ryder. How may I help you?"

"This is Rita Brockman at the *New York Times*. I'm calling about your new *U.S. & World Atlas*."

"Oh, very good."

"It's very handsome and very informative. It looks very easy to use."

"Thank you."

"But there is one problem."

"Oh?"

"The state of Montana's missing."

"I beg your pardon."

"Montana's missing."

"Can't be. A couple of pages must've stuck together."

"No. I've gone through page by page. The numbers are in sequence and all the states are there except Montana."

"You bought a defective copy. I'll have another one sent by messenger today."

"I've looked at five copies. They're all the same."

"You're from the *New York Times*?"

"Yes."

"How do I know that?"

"You can call the general number here and ask for me. Or I can give you my direct line."

"I'm going to look at a copy of the atlas. Someone will get back to you."

Jonathan Ryder hung up. Thirty seconds later he was standing outside the office of Alicia Powers, head of Grand Tally's corporate communications. He leaned in. "Ms. Powers. Something's come up."

Alicia turned away from her computer screen.

"I just got a call from the *New York Times*. A something Brockman who said Montana's missing from the new atlas."

"Yeah, right."

"I don't think it was a prank."

At that moment Abby Pearlman stepped up to the office and said, "We got a problem, folks. We've gotten eight calls this morning about the new atlas. Three people have said the state of Montana was omitted. Guess what? It was."

"Oh, my God," said Powers, and sat in disbelief.

Ryder turned to Pearlman and said, "The *New York Times* just said the same."

All Pearlman could say was, "Shit."

"I want to see it for myself," Powers said, and reached for a copy of the atlas that sat on her bookshelf. She opened it and skimmed through to the M's. Maine—turn a page—Maryland—turn a page—Michigan—turn a page—Minnesota—turn a page—Nebraska. She turned the paper between her thumb and forefinger to make sure two pages were not sticking together, then turned back. Minnesota.

"Christ," she said, and got on the phone to Leslie Driggs. "We've got a crisis, Mr. Driggs. I've got to see you immediately. Better have Mr. Feinstein there too." Then she was up and carrying the atlas with her down the hall.

7.

Shortly after noon Lorene's bag was packed and she was standing by the porch rail, wondering what had become of her brother and sister-in-law. And where was Buck? Had the men already gone after Lew Mitchell? She was taking deep drags on a cigarette, hearing the windmill clatter and looking both ways down the road for a dust cloud that would signal their arrival.

This was the fourth day after Charlie and Olivia had left Chicago. Buck was wrong. It did not take four days to drive from there to here. Something had happened. She went inside and called her brother's home. The answering machine came on. She left a brief message, then called the Montana State Patrol, giving them a description of Charlie and Olivia and saying their car had Illinois plates. The state patrol gave her the number for the South Dakota and Minnesota State Police. She called them too. Then she went to the refrigerator and got a bottle of beer and went back to the porch and sat down and lit a cigarette. Something was wrong.

CHAPTER FOUR

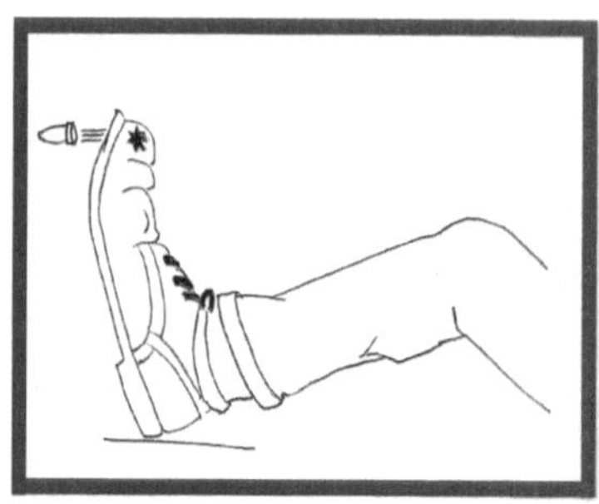

Siggy Harris had managed to pull Kline inside an abandoned dugout on the slope above the Remos' house. The dugout had been the temporary abode of a homesteader a hundred years before, a tiny place eight feet long, five feet wide, and four feet deep. A three-foot wall rose above the ground, covered by a roof. The wood was rotting and the dugout was cramped and filled with trash, but the agents had set up their bugging devices, tape recorder, and telescope inside.

"Ooohhhhhhh!!!!" Kline wailed, "It's my foot! My fuckin' foot!"

"Shot your foot?"

"You shot it, asshole!"

"I didn't shoot your fuckin' foot, you did. You fell and your gun went off."

"So did yours, after you tripped on me."

"Yeah, but I didn't shoot you. I couldn'tve. I fell with my arms stretched out in front of me. I fired towards the house."

"Those fuckin' freaks got two hostages, man, and you have to fuck up and fall over me."

"You fell."

"I was throwing myself into position!"

"Oh, yeah, right."

"Man, I'll see that you get a desk job for life. In some shitty rat hole somewhere in the desert. You bet your sweet ass I will."

"You fuckin' tripped so don't fuckin' try to blame me. I bet those reporters got it on tape too."

"Ohhh, shit! I forgot about those mothers. Where are they?"

Harris looked out the front. "I don't see 'em."

"If you see 'em, shoot 'em."

"Right, I'm gonna kill some guy from the *New York Times*. Just say when."

"Don't get fuckin' fresh, Harris, you shot my foot. Help me get this goddamned shoe off so I can see how bad it is."

Kline sat on the dirt floor of the dugout, holding up his left leg and foot. His shoe was covered with blood.

"Oh, shit," Harris said, looking at it.

"Get the fuckin' shoe off and get this foot bandaged. Stop the bleeding."

Harris unlaced Kline's shoe and began, gently, to take it off.

"Stop it! Stop it!" Kline yelled. Harris let go of the foot and Kline snapped, "You moron, you tryin' to kill me?"

"Got a knife?"

"Got a razor blade somewhere."

Harris rummaged through a canvas bag and pulled out a single-edged razor blade and started cutting off Kline's shoe. A half hour later, after much bickering and snarling, Harris had the shoe off and Kline's foot bandaged. The bleeding was bad. Kline had shot off his big toe and nothing the two men could do was stopping the flow of blood.

"Get the tape rollin'," Kline said. "Let's hear what the Remos got to say and make a record for Washington. Then let's get out of here. I gotta get to a hospital."

"I'll call for an ambulance."

Harris switched on the recorder before picking up his cellular phone and punched 911. A recording came on saying, "Please check your number and dial again." Harris impatiently punched in the three numbers once again and got the same recording.

"It's not working," he told Kline. "We're in a valley. I'll talk to those reporters." Harris poked his head out of the dugout looking for signs of life from the house, looked up the hill to the trees where the reporters stood and judged the distance. One hundred fifty, maybe two hundred feet. Up a steep slope with no cover. "Say a prayer," he mumbled as he clambered out.

As Harris scrambled up the hill, he saw several cameramen record his run. "Bastards," he thought, and his anger gave him an extra burst of speed. When he reached the journalists, they surrounded him with microphones in hand, all asking questions simultaneously.

"What happened?"

"How's your partner?"

"What're your plans now?"

"Have you made contact with the Remos?"

"Get the fuck away from me!" he said, pushing away the microphones. "if you don't put down those cameras and recorders, you'll be arrested for impeding an investigation. Got it?"

A producer pushed to the front of the crowd, asking, "What's the problem?"

"I need a phone. Fast."

"Okay," she said, "Let's go over here." She led him to a van with the microwave antennae raised and handed him a phone.

Harris punched 911 and a girl's voice answered: "Hello?"

"I'm calling from off of Highway 25 on . . . just a second." He turned to the producer. "What's the name of this road?"

"I don't know," she said, then turned to the others and called: "Does anyone know the name of this road?"

"It's County Road R15," Gus Harvey said.

"County Road R15," Harris told the girl.

"And what's the problem?" the girl asked.

"We need an ambulance. There's been a shooting. A man's big toe has been shot off and he's bleeding badly."

"Is there anyone there to administer first aid?" the girl asked.

"Yes," Harris said, beginning to lose patience. "I administered first aid."

"And what's your name?"

"Just get an ambulance here!"

"Please stay calm, sir. We'll have an ambulance there within the hour."

"Within an hour!? He may bleed to death by then!"

"Please stay calm, sir."

"Look! Just get a fucking ambulance here with a medic crew that can handle the problem!"

"Sir, there's no need to get abusive and use foul language," she said in an even tone. "I'm just doing my job. I don't make the rules. I can't make the ambulances go any faster."

Harris interrupted her. "Listen! Will you listen to me!? I am with the FBI. The wounded man is also FBI. We are under fire! We need an ambulence and police backup! DO YOU UNDERSTAND?"

A moment later Harris was holding a dead phone.

2.

The girl who had answered Harris's 911 call was Celia Roberts, a nineteen-year-old graduate of Moosehead High who was sitting in for the regular police dispatcher, her mother, Stacy Roberts. Celia had done this only once before and had no training in handling 911 calls. Especially crank 911 calls like that last one.

The dispatch radio was in the Rosebud County sheriff's office in downtown Moosehead. With a population under 2,000, Moosehead was not rich enough to afford, or large enough to warrant, buying a dispatch radio for the sheriff's office and another for the police station. All emergency calls, including fire, ambulance, and police, were directed to the one location.

When Harris called again, thirty seconds later, she said: "Mister, I'm warning you, I'm going to trace your call and you're going to be sorry," and hung up for the second time.

When her mother returned thirty minutes later, Celia said, "I just had a crank on the phone. Claimed to be FBI. He was real rude and swore like a gangster."

Stacy shook her head and said, "You have to learn to live with those types. They're everywhere today. Anyway, thanks for covering for me."

"Okay," Celia said on her way to the door.

3.

By three o'clock Eastern Standard Time, Grand Tally CEO Leslie Driggs and CFO Leonard Feinstein were discussing the new atlas and the missing state. Anticipating returns from oil companies (which had purchased tens of thousands of copies for gas station convenience stores) and calls from the media across the country (calling for an explanation), Ms. Powers had immediately called the two men and advised a strategic planning session. Feinstein and Driggs were now staring at Powers, trying to comprehend how this horrible mistake could have occurred. They looked at each other and back to Powers.

"Let me see if I have this right, Ms. Powers," said Mr. Driggs. "Only after the atlas was completed did Mr. Mason and his accounting team realize there were two additional pages."

"That is correct."

"Nobody, apparently, did a preliminary run-through in the planning stage."

"Not that I am aware of."

"And then Mr. Mason and his team, after realizing their error, instead of having a map or two redrawn, or consulting us, simply decided to eliminate Montana."

"Apparently so," said Ms. Powers.

"Why?" asked Mr. Driggs.

"I can't say."

Mr. Driggs looked at Mr. Feinstein. "We need to call in Macintosh, Hadley & Smith." Macintosh, Hadley & Smith was a well-known public relations firm specializing in crisis management.

"I'll call them immediately," said Ms. Powers. "I suggest we ask them to send John Bury, if he's available."

"Good choice," said Driggs. He looked at Feinstein and grinned. "Bury's so slick he could turn a triple tanker oil spill into a P.R. opportunity."

Feinstein chuckled and nodded in agreement. "I remember two years ago when 5,000 pounds of beef at Blubber Packing was contaminated with salmonella and killed thirty-two people.

Bury shifted the blame onto two Mexican workers. Remember? He actually got criminal charges filed against them." Feinstein laughed. "That guy's a genius."

Ms. Powers stood. "I'll get on it right away."

Feinstein gave her the thumbs up sign. "Go out there," he said, "and lick ass!"

She flashed a smile and walked quickly out of the meeting room to her office, where she called George Hadley, who told her that John Bury was on assignment, but added: "I don't think your problem's serious. I've got a dozen specialists who can turn this around in short order. I'll send you Monica Clapper and Thornton Granger. They finished an assignment in L.A. this morning and are on their way back. I can have them at your office tomorrow."

"We need someone now, George. We need strategic planning this afternoon."

"I'll see if I can reach them en route. I'll call you back."

Thirty minutes later George Hadley called to say that Granger and Clapper would arrive at Grand Tally offices late that afternoon.

4.

As Ms. Powers hung up her phone, Arlan Brandt, Sheriff of Rosebud County was driving along Highway 25 when he spotted a 1995 Buick Regal with out-of-state plates parked on the shoulder of the westbound lane. He pulled over and walked to the driver's door and tried opening it. Locked. He looked inside. Empty, with no sign of damage. He walked around the car and saw a tiny piece of paper under the windshield on which was printed: "Ran out of gas. Be back soon."

When had they left the note? How long had the vehicle been there? He went back to his car, made a note in his logbook, put a tag on the Buick's windshield and left.

5.

Lorene, still on her front porch, wondered at her husband's whereabouts. She called Jeannie again.

"Jeannie, it's me, Lorene. I have no idee where Buck is. You heard anything?"

"No. Why should I?"

Jeannie was married to Bouncer, who at this moment was standing next to Buck on Cap's ranch, passing Buck a bottle.

"Buck left here earlier today with Cap and Byron," Lorene told her. "They was all burnt up over the fact that Sheriff Brandt arrested Lew Mitchell fer shootin' at sumbody."

"Yeah . . . . . So?"

"I thought maybe they'd come by an' got Bouncer. They said they was gonna round up the gang."

"I ain't seen 'em and I ain't seen Bouncer since breakfast."

"Well, shoot. I'm worried, frankly."

"Well, they're just drinkin' somewhere, same as usual. They'll be back. Listen, I gotta pack. If we gotta be in Billings in two hours, I better come over real soon."

"Okay, see ya."

"Bye."

But the nagging feeling that Buck and the others might have gotten in a scrape, or were about to, did not leave her.

6.

Cap and Sonny worked five hours that day transferring the group's guns, ammunition, and artillery to an abandoned line-shack on Cap's ranch. The others guarded the original (and now slowly diminishing) cache and spent their time divvying up a case of beer and passing around a bottle of Jim Beam as they practiced target shooting.

Byron Pulver tossed away a can of beer and lifted his Colt .45 and flipped open the cylinder, wavering as he slowly pushed bullets into its chambers. "So we got us a fuckin' gov'mint spy."

"Byron," said Buck, "I don't think we do. 'Sides, Cap jus'

said it was a possibility."

"If it wasn't an inside job, how the hell did they find Sonny's cache?"

"Everybody knows Sonny hunts," said Alfred.

They had been debating this subject ever since they first heard about the theft, three hours ago.

"Well, whoever it is," said Byron, "is gonna get a slug right between the eyebrows. Blam!" He lifted his revolver, aimed at a beer can and fired, then looked around at the group.

"Byron," said Bouncer, a big man with a ten-gallon hat and a shotgun, "ain't no one here ratted."

"I don't think so, either," said Alfred.

"Hell," said Buck, "we've known each other thirty, forty years. We growd up with each other."

"That don't mean spit," answered Byron. "Blood don't mean spit, nuther." And Byron spat.

He was shorter than the others, but he talked more and louder than they did. He liked to pick fights with bigger men when he was drunk or with a friend. Byron was good at starting fights at Sidewinders. He liked to take off his belt and wrap it around his fist with the buckle up front, go up to a stranger in the bar and with no provocation whatsoever haul off and smash the fellow in the face. He had won a few fights by the virtue of surprise but early on had gotten himself whipped more times than he cared to remember. He soon learned to pick his fights only when Sonny or Bouncer were there to pitch in.

Byron lifted his revolver again and aimed at a beer can, wavered, and fired. The bullet struck a rock and ricocheted towards Pee Wee Bowers, cut a hole in Pee Wee's trouser legs, and dug into the ground, spitting up dirt.

"Yow!!!!" Pee Wee yelled. "Watch it, man!"

"Watch it what?" Byron demanded. "You walked into that fuckin' bullet. Watch yerself."

Fifty yards away, on the rim of a rise, two figures lay hidden behind clumps of grama grass. If the Montana Militia had seen them, they would have recognized the Indian and the cowboy from Sidewinders. These two observers could see a short man, whom they recognized as Byron Pulver, waver towards the one called "Pee Wee." They saw another man, carrying a shotgun, walking behind Byron.

"Yer too drunk to shoot!" Pee Wee yelled.

"I ain't drunk," said Byron, squinting and frowning. "And yer a fuckin' liar."

"Byron . . . . . !!!" cautioned Pee Wee.

"You stepped right in the way of my shot! Did ya see that?" he said, turning to the others for confirmation. "He stepped right into my fuckin'' shot, then says I'm drunk! Bull fuckin' shit!" Then he noticed Bouncer standing behind him. "What are you standing in back of me for? Step away! Git!"

Bouncer, gripping his shotgun with both hands, swung upwards, knocking the gun stock against the side of Byron's head, then watched Byron collapse without a sound.

Pee Wee let out a rush of air. "Thanks."

"He's fuckin' crazier 'n ever," said Alfred.

"He woulda shot me," said Pee Wee.

"He mighta," said Bouncer.

"Jeez, he's gonna be sore at you," Alfred said to Bouncer.

"I ain't afraid of him," Bouncer said.

Just then they heard the sound of an engine and soon they saw a pickup racing towards them. When the pickups stopped, Cap and Sonny jumped out.

"All right," said Cap, "that's it. She's done."

"Cap," said Buck, "Byron got a little squirrelly and Bouncer had to coldcock him."

"Yeah, he went off," said Alfred.

"I was afraid he was gonna shoot me," Pee Wee said.

"He just might do that to someone some day," Cap agreed. "We gotta get rid of him."

"You mean . . . . ????" Alfred started.

"No, no," said Cap, "I mean cut him from the group."

"I think we oughta," said Bouncer.

"Dump 'im on my flatbed for now," Cap said.

Alfred and Pee Wee carried Byron to Cap's truck. The rest of the men loaded the remaining arms and ammunition onto the flatbeds of the three trucks.

"What we're gonna do now," said Cap, "is spring Lew Mitchell."

"Whoooooeeeee!" someone yelled.

"Atta boy, Cap!" someone else shouted.

"All riiiiiiiggghhhht!!!!!!!!" Alfred cried.

"This is the one thing that Byron was lookin' forward to tonight," said Sonny.

"He'll be there," said Cap, "only he won't be watchin', he'll be out!"

The men howled with laughter.

"One last thing," Cap said. "Pullin' Lew Mitchell outa jail's just the first step we gotta take on a loooonng trip.We're gonna find out who's behind eliminatin' Montana. We're gonna put a stop to it, no matter what it takes or who it takes OUT!"

"YaHOOOOO!!!!" the men yelled.

"Get in yer trucks, men!" Cap called. "Make sure each of ya's got a rifle and ammo. Let's PULL OUT!!!"

The men shouted and whooped as they raced for their cars and trucks. Then Buck pulled up short and shouted: "Where we goin'?"

Most of the others pulled up short, too, stopped with their hands on their door handles.

"Yeah, where?" shouted Sonny.

"The sheriff's office!" shouted Cap. "Where the hell d'ya think?"

"AllRIGHT!!!!!!" everyone shouted and jumped in their cars and trucks.

As soon as the men rattled off in a cloud of dust, the two men who had been hiding behind the rim of the hill stood up. Alan Bird, a Mescalero Apache, and Ez Lawson, a lawyer, worked for a secret and very small agency within the Department of Homeland Security. Its secrecy was such that few people, including the President of the United States, knew of its existence. One circumstance that made this possible was the fact that the agency's twelve full-time employees were all off the books. The majority of people working for it were independent contractors and paid cash.

Bird and Lawson, both independent contractors, had been following various militia groups in eastern Montana for the last half-year. As they wrote back in one report, they considered the Moosehead outfit "mostly a lot of talkers." Still, they had stolen the weapons at Sonny's arms cache, because, they noted, "Several of these men, including Byron Pulver, George "Cap" Matlock and Jerry "Bouncer" Peters appear capable of public acts of terrorism and bear watching." In the course of the theft, Bird had torn his red shirt on Sonny's barbed wire fence, leaving the militiamen a bit of evidence to misinterpret.

7.

It was three o'clock Mountain States Time when Jeannie pulled up in the Simpson's drive. Lorene was sitting on the porch smoking a cigarette and drinking a beer, with a suitcase next to her. She threw her head back, chugged the rest of the bottle and slammed it on the small table. After throwing her suitcase in the back of the pickup and seating herself next to Jeannie, her friend said, "Aren't you forgettin' somethin'?"

"What?" Lorene asked, annoyed.

"My beer."

"I gotta go back in the house and get you a beer?"

"Well you been drinkin' 'em all day, I can tell. I only had me two. How do you expect me to make it to Billings?"

"Why don't you just drive. Stop at the 7-11 in Moosehead and I'll get a sixpack."

"I need a beer now."

"Oh, shit."

Lorene got out of the pickup, disappeared inside the house and returned with three bottles. Jeannie put the pickup in gear and took off.

"That's more like it," Jeannie said. "How about openin' me one?"

"It's not enough that I had to go back in the house and get you a beer, now I gotta open it for you. Want me t' drink it for ya too?"

"Lorene, how about cannin' the wise stuff, just give me a goddamn bottle."

"Piss, piss, piss," Lorene said.

"How the hell do you expect me to give you moral support if I'm sober?"

"Well, that's true."

"Goddamn right it's true."

Lorene flipped off the bottle cap and Jeannie took a sip.

"Damn! This is gonna be fun."

"Ain't it?" Lorene said. "I'm gonna fix their wagons."

"Correction: we're gonna fix their wagons!"

The two ladies clinked bottles and roared with laughter, headed towards Moosehead and the road to Billings.

CHAPTER FIVE

In the Grand Tally offices, employees in Mr. Mason's department fidgeted all day as they wondered when the ax would fall. There were whispered conversations by the water coolers and in the restrooms. Each of them blamed his problems on Alvina Rates, "whose big mouth and arrogant manner," said Mr. Potts, "had caused this national uproar. If that clumsy monster had not antagonized the Montana hillbilly no one would have paid the slightest attention to the omission." Of one thing everyone was certain: that some or all of them would be fired. Most spent the day, when they could concentrate long enough, searching the want ads on the Internet.

At four thirty-five, Thornton Granger and Monica Clapper arrived from Macintosh, Hadley & Smith. At four thirty-seven they were seated in the director's meeting room with Mr. Feinstein, Mr. Driggs, and Ms. Powers.

"Thank you for coming so promptly," Mr. Feinstein said.

"You have a problem," said Mr. Granger, "we're here to fix it. Please give us all the details."

Mr. Feinstein gave the details, and finished with, "First off, we're going to fire Potts and his losers."

"We'll fix it so they'll never get a job. Anywhere. Ever," said Driggs. "And since Rates is the one who went on TV, we'll make her the scapegoat. Feed her to the media."

"Whoaa! Whooa! Whoaa!" Granger interjected. "Bad idea."

"Terrible idea," Clapper said.

"Scapegoat your own people? And fire them too?" Granger was astounded. "That's just like going on national television and admitting you screwed up. No, no, no, no. That's an apology!"

"Just like an apology," chimed Clapper.

"Let these people keep their jobs, for the time being," said Granger. "Six months, eight months from now start phasing them out, yank their pensions, do whatever you want. But not now, not until this is forgotten."

"In two months this will be forgotten," Clapper added.

"In the meantime," said Granger, "we have to consider your options. Number one is the public apology, but we've ruled that out. Number two is to issue a press release telling the world that the atlas is fine as it is, but that you'll print an addendum. You'll do separate maps of the state of Montana and the U.S. and sell them at cost to anyone who requests a copy. The third option is for Grand Tally to appear a victim. I advise you to pursue options two and three."

"Yes," said Clapper, "but the essence of saving the situation, in my opinion, is to make Grand Tally appear the victim."

"How the hell can you do that?" Driggs wanted to know.

Feinstein leaned forward in his chair, eyes wide, mouth open in expectation.

"That's what we'll have to figure," said Granger. "Any ideas Monica?"

"Not yet. But something's cooking."

"Well, I have one," Granger said. "Options two and three are one and the same. First off, you'll say your editors checked the blue line proofs and Montana was there. And the U.S. map was there. Next thing you know, when the atlas arrives, Montana's missing and the U.S. map is a piece of junk."

"You read my mind," said Clapper. "Just what I was thinking."

"You didn't screw up, someone else did," said Granger.

"Guess who?" asked Clapper.

"Yes? Yes? Who?" Feinstein demanded.

Clapper opened her arms, palms upward as though revealing the mystery. "The printers."

"The printers deleted the two pages of the digital file that contained Montana," Granger said.

"They're the screwups," Clapper added.

"Total incompetents."

"Morons."

"Bums."

"Idiots."

Driggs and Feinstein smiled and looked at each other. Ms. Powers was lost in admiration.

"But that's not the end of it," Granger continued.

"Not by a long shot," said Clapper.

"You will print an addendum—the state map. And anyone who wants a copy of it can have it at cost."

"Don't forget a corrected version of the U.S. map," said Clapper. "You'll print that too and sell it at cost."

"Best of all," added Granger, offering the piece de resistance, "You're suing the printers."

"But how do we explain the screwed-up U.S. map?"

"The printers are responsible for that too. Had to be. Sheer maliciousness, whatever. Who knows why. You're hiring an agency to investigate the reasons and get to the bottom of it."

Feinstein and Driggs sank back in their chairs, all tension suddenly drained. Then they were laughing.

"Tomorrow morning you'll announce a press conference for one o'clock," said Granger. "There you'll outline the real cause of the problem and announce your law suit."

"Oh, that's brilliant," said Ms. Powers.

"Thank you," said Granger.

"I think we can add to that," said Clapper. "You must announce that once you win the suit, the proceeds will be donated to the Montana public schools. And the Montana Sioux Indians. Terrible poverty there."

"I like that," said Feinstein.

"Yes, indeed," said Driggs. "Ms. Powers, prepare a press release."

"Yes, sir. At once."

As Ms. Powers left the room, the newly created philanthropists, Driggs and Feinstein, smiled to each other.

2.

As the mapmakers and the crisis managemnt team discussed how they might turn Grand Tally's problems to its advantage, Siggy Harris was still in the trailer, talking to the producer. "Listen," he told her. "My partner needs medical attention bad. Someone's gotta drive him to a hospital."

"God knows where the nearest one is," she said.

All this time Gus Harvey had his cameraman film the interchange between Harris and the producer.

"Call 911 and ask," Harris said, almost frantically.

He moved to the cluster of journalists, picked the one who looked the strongest and said, "You're gonna help me. We're going back to that dugout and get my partner and carry him out. Got it?"

The reporter looked down the hill, thought about the long distance and said, "I got a family."

"My partner's wounded and might bleed to death!" Harris countered.

The man shrugged.

Harris looked at another man, who said, "I couldn't make that climb carrying someone, I've got asthma."

"I'd help," said another, "but I've got a bad back."

Others just shook their heads and started moving away.

"If he dies," Harris threatened all of them, "you sonsofbitches will answer for it."

The reporters ad cameramen kept walking away.

"I'll try 911 again," the producer said.

3.

An hour after he had inspected the Traverses' car, Sheriff Arlan Brandt was driving toward it once again. After looking for signs that the owners had returned, he called the station.

"Come in, headquarters."

"Headquarters here," said Stacy Stevens.

"Stacy, this is Arlan. I'm on Highway 25, twenty miles west of Moosehead. We've got a vehicle in the westbound lane. It's been here an hour. Do you have any report on it?"

"What's the car, make, and license plate?"

"Buick Regal, Illinois license ARJ 189."

"Buick Regal, Illinois plate ARJ 189."

"Correct."

"I'll check."

Brandt clicked off. Five minutes later Stacy called back.

"That Buick Regal belongs to Charles Travers of Chicago, Illinois. That's Buck Simpson's brother-in-law. His wife Lorene called this morning, saying her brother and sister-in-law were long overdue. Hadn't arrived."

"Put out an APB on them."

"Will do."

"Get hold of the Simpsons. Get a description of the in-laws. Give me their names again."

"Charles Travers."

"Do you have the wife's name?"

"Negative."

Sheriff Brandt stepped out of his car and took another look at the Travers' vehicle. He saw no damage to the car or spots of blood or bits of clothing that would indicate a struggle. He went back to his car, got a flat metal bar, and pushed it down one of the Travers' windows. He hooked the lock and yanked it up. The door opened and Brandt slid inside. He opened the glove compartment, looking for papers or anything else that might yield a clue to what had happened. He searched their luggage. Clothes, camera, a few paperbacks. A cooler with pop and sandwiches.

Back in his car Brandt thought about their note: "Gone for gas. Be back soon." Had they run out of gas and gotten a ride, or was that note written by an assailant? Just then Stacy came back on the radio.

"All units. There's a call for help. A man identifying himself as an FBI agent reports a standoff with kidnappers."

FBI, Brandt thought. You bet. The FBI would've notified him if they were in his bailiwick. Or would they? Maybe not.

Stacy was saying: "Hostage situation in progress in Wheeler Township off County Road X15. The Randall Place. All units, please respond. Five-one."

"Five-one here. This could be a crank call but let's proceed."

"Five-two?"

"Five-two."

"Five-three?"

"Five-three."

"Proceed immediately to the Randall Place off County Road X15."

Sheriff Brandt tore off.

4.

Inside the Remos' house, Mrs. Travers was lying on a sofa, stirring and moaning. Her husband sat by her side, holding her hand and alternately looking from her to the Remos, some of whom were peeking out the windows from behind curtains.

"Do you see anything?" asked Mrs. Clingmeier, kneeling at a back window.

"No," said Reverend Angle, looking out a front window.

"Who were they?" Letta asked, "and why were they shooting at us?"

"The Day of Judgment has come," intoned the reverend.

"I heard one of them shout 'FBI,'" said Mrs. Clingmeier.

"I heard 'FBI' too," said George Slow Bear.

"Why were they shootin' at us?" Charles Dinkins wondered.

"Do you think they were FBI?" someone else asked.

"How could they be FBI if they was firing at us?" asked the reverend. "They wasn't FBI. They are the troops of the Antichrist. The countdown for the final day has begun."

"Amen," the Remos intoned quietly.

"Praise Jesus that we have been chosen to witness the End,

chosen to see the arrival of our Lord in the days of final glory," said the reverend.

"Praise Jesus," said Mrs. Dinkins, and the others added, "Amen."

"The final battle for possession of the world will be fought right here, in this house. That is why the Lord brought us here, to re-enact His sacrifice in the Final Drama."

"Are we called for martyrdom, reverend?" asked Charles Dinkins.

"Judging by the presence of the armed force outside, there can be no doubt. Yes, Charles, we are to wear the martyr's cloak of glory."

"Amen," said Carl.

"Praise Jesus," said Mrs. Clingmeier.

Mr. and Mrs. Dinkins began quietly singing an old Negro spiritual.

"Does God want us to fight these devils, reverend?" George Slow Bear asked. "Just say the word."

"I will ask Him," the reverend said and knelt in the middle of the room, hands clasped and head bowed.

5.

Stacey was back at the switchboard when the network news producer called again. The situation was explained convincingly and an ambulance was dispatched from Moosehead. Meanwhile agent Harris called Hardwicke at bureau headquarters. "What's up?" Hardwicke asked.

"The Remos just nabbed a man and woman, dragged the couple inside."

"Kidnapped?"

"No question. I need backup."

"Call the sheriff."

"We called. We're waiting to hear."

"I'll send sharpshooters."

"Kline's been hit."

"Bad?"

"In the foot. Lotta bleedin. I've called an ambulance. When will those sharpshooters be here?"

"Tomorrow morning."

They hung up. Harris ran back to the dugout while Hardwicke called the bureau's director, Jay Ritchie. Ritchie was a lifelong bureaucrat with many influential friends in government. The previous year he had avoided Senate censure for the deaths of twenty-four people—none with criminal records—who had been killed by agents in unusual encounters. The bureau's critics had labeled these deaths murders. The deceased included five disabled and unemployed Vietnam veterans who had been living in an apartment in a rundown section of Chicago.

A bureau informant tagged them drug dealers with ties to Al Qaeda. An FBI swat team surrounded their apartment building and the agent in charge talked through a loud speaker, demanding that the veterans throw their weapons out the window and walk outside with hands up. Since three of the five veterans were paraplegics this was impossible.

The veterans, however, never heard the demands, only loud noises. According to witnesses, when one veteran appeared at a window, the firing commenced. Someone, somehow, set the building on fire, killing not only the five veterans but a Mexican woman and her three children. In the Senate investigation that followed, it was determined that the mother had set the fire. Witnesses came forward who said that she had frequently beaten her children and yelled at them nightly. They stated that she and the veterans were smuggling cocaine, selling it, and sending the profits to the Al Qaeda. The vets, witnesses said, had violent tempers and had made numerous threats against neighbors. For the FBI's quick action, Ritchie had not only avoided censure but had earned commendations for himself and the bureau.

Now Hardwicke was on the phone with Ritchie, explaining the situation. "One of our men is down with a smashed knee and foot. We've got one remaining agent there holding off the Remos. The situation is critical. I need another ten, twenty agents down there now."

"You got it," said Ritchie, who alerted FBI tactical units

in St. Louis, San Francisco, Seattle, Los Angeles, and Minneapolis—in all ordering 150 agents (including two dozen sharp shooters) to fly to Billings, Montana immediately, with enough arms and armor for a drawn-out siege. His orders: shoot to kill. "They've crippled one agent whose partner is holding off the mob. If we don't get them help within the hour, they won't make it. Get down there and use all necessary force to neutralize the Remos."

Within minutes, 150 FBI agents were donning bulletproof vests and pulling AK-47s out of rifle racks, stuffing gun bags full of ammunition, and heading for army airports.

6.

In the road beyond the Remos' house, cameramen had set up tripods. Some were filming the dugout, hoping for a shot of the agents; others kept their cameras focused on the house, waiting for a face to appear at a window. The reporters, meanwhile, were busy: some in their vans writing stories; others reading stories into cellular phones to newsroom employees who typed them into computers; still others were sending unedited footage by microwave to New York.

The most prestigious newsman present, Gus Harvey, was now grooming himself in front of the camera. At six o'clock Eastern Standard Time, David Whortley, CDC network news anchor, went on the air.

"Good evening. Tonight's top story: Death in Montana. America's most notorious Christian cult, the Remos, today settled in a home outside Moosehead, Montana. But almost immediately the gang found itself engaged in a shootout with the FBI. Correspondent Gus Harvey reports."

The screen flashed to Harvey, looking concerned, standing on the road above the Remos' house.

"Good evening, David. Tragedy struck Moosehead, Montana four hours ago when twelve members of the charismatic Christian cult, the Remos, gunned down an FBI agent attempting to rescue a man and woman from their clutches. That began one of the most grisly shoot-outs in recent memory." Turning, Harvey pointed at the Remos' house.

"Can you tell us anything about the kidnapped couple?" Whortley asked.

"We don't know their names. All we can say with certainty is that they were forcibly dragged inside this house."

As Harvey spoke, the screen showed footage of Kline and Harris lying on the slope facing the Remos who were clustered in front of their home. Then a close-up on the Remos. A gunshot. The camera panned to Kline and Harris, sprawled on the ground.

Meanwhile Harvey was saying, "Two shots were fired, after which the Remos entered their hideout."

The screen displayed footage of the Remos squeezing through the front door.

"One of the agents," Harvey was saying, "was clearly wounded."

"Do you know which of the Remos fired that shot?" Whortley asked.

"No, David, we don't. Without an expert looking carefully at this footage, it's impossible to tell which of the cultists wounded the agent."

"How is he?"

"That's the horrible part of it, David. We just don't know. The agents, understandably, have kept reporters at a distance, and we don't even know their names. Right now they are holed up in a dugout of some sort past those trees"—Harvey turned and pointed—"over there."

The camera panned to the trees.

Whortley asked, "Have you seen any movement from inside the house?"

"No, we haven't. And that raises the most important question of all: What will the Remos do with their hostages? That is what everyone is asking: What will the Remos do next? The tension here is unbelievable."

"Thank you, Gus. We'll be checking with you periodically."

The screen filled with a head shot of Whortley who said, "That was CDC correspondent Gus Harvey in Moosehead, Montana."

7.

After lunch Rex and Sally Lou sat in Jelton's office as he told them, "Look, I have this perfect idea. I've booked relatives of the Remos for tomorrow."

"We're not a human interest show," Rex interjected. "We do celebrity interviews."

"I know, but this is your chance to show your compassionate sides."

"Like whadda we do?"

"We put the relatives in chairs in a semicircle and have both of you to the side, asking questions about their trapped relatives."

"I thought their relatives were supposed to be loonies. They practically killed an FBI agent. We're supposed to feel sorry for them?"

"That's it! Exactly. Here are these fourteen lost souls who think their leader hears the voice of God. Fourteen lost souls who have put themselves in the hands of a crazed maniac. I want you to bring out the human dra-a-a-ma ."

"Have you canceled three celebrity interviews for THIS?" Rex screeched.

"YES!!!! Yes! Yes! Yes! Who is the biggest film star today compared with the tortured souls inside that cabin . . . or house, or whatever it is."

"Do you realize," said Rex, "that yesterday we were yelling at a woman in Montana telling her she was a liar for claiming she lived in Montana. We agreed with that moron from Grand Tally that Montana didn't exist! Now we're saying it not only exists, but that we actually care about fourteen losers trapped inside a house who have killed an FBI agent?"

"Yes!"

"You've lost your mind. If you ever had one!"

"Please stop yelling, both of you," pleaded Sally Lou. "I'm getting a headache."

"All right. Sorry," Jelton said. "We'll discuss this reasonably."

"Thank you," Sally Lou said quietly.

"This is the P.R. opportunity of a lifetime. Do you see?"

"No."

"Why are we thinking about P.R.?" asked Sally Lou. "I just want to forget about that whole horrible mess yesterday. I don't want a bunch of horrid misfits with overbites sitting ten feet away from me. We don't even know if they're carrying some disgusting virus."

"Look," reasoned Jelton, "anyone who watched yesterday's show knows we made a mistake. We claimed—correction, you claimed—that Montana didn't exist. Twenty million women with nothing to do heard you say it."

"You said it didn't exist too," Rex snapped.

"Please," Sally Lou whimpered.

"Okay," said Jelton. "You're right. I said it too. Now we're going to claim, at the start of tomorrow's show, that we thought the whole Montana bit was a gag. Obviously Montana's a state. We knew that from grade school. We assumed that that Rates woman had the map made just for the gag, and that the caller was in on it."

"I like that," Rex said.

"I don't want to think about it," said Sally Lou.

"You don't have to do any thinking," said Jelton. "Let Rex do the talking tomorrow. You just look compassionate."

"Which of the relatives are coming?" Rex asked.

"One of the Remos is a Sioux Indian, and we have his sister. This guy used to be a boozer, until he found Jesus. His sister left the reservation years ago. Now she's a clerk for United Airlines. She says he's a real loser. Never wanted to leave the reservation. Until he found Jesus.

"And we got the ninety-year-old mother of the black man. I could barely understand her when I spoke with her yesterday. She's lost half her teeth. She was crying her poor old heart out on the phone."

"So whadda we want a mumbling old crybaby on the show for?"

Jelton explained slowly. "We want to hear her beg her son and daughter-in-law to leave the cabin. And take their medicine. She's an old Aunty Tom Baptist goodie two-shoes. She'll cry her eyes out. She'll be great."

"I can't wait," Rex said in disgust. "I don't need to know any more. I don't want to know any more."

"Re-e-e-e-x-x-x, it'll be great," Jelton said. "You'll see. I'll give you both a profile of the guests and each of the Remos, plus a dozen questions. You can wing the rest."

"Beautiful." Rex shook his head.

"Plus you'll have a short speech at the top of the show that you'll read off the teleprompter. About how we were duped, how we thought the whole thing was a gag. And that we're demanding an apology from Grand Tally for causing us and our viewers such pain and embarrassment."

"That I like," said Rex.

"Attaboy!" Jelton said encouragingly.

"I'm going to be sick," said Sally Lou.

CHAPTER SIX

If we were on a very large crane that could lift us several miles above Rosebud County and we had very good glasses, here is what we would see: three sheriff's department vehicles racing from different parts of the county to converge on the Randall Place. Two of the cars are speeding along gravel roads, leaving trails of dust in their wakes. The third car, Sheriff Brandt's, is racing along Highway 25 toward County Road X15. From our crane we also see four pickups and two cars filled with members of the Montana Militia roaring south along County Road R2T and about to turn onto Highway 25. As Sheriff Brandt races past County Road R2T, headed east, the pickups and cars roar up to it and veer west on the highway, headed for Moosehead.

Moving our line of sight to the east we see a car with two women headed south, towards Billings. Each is thinking about New York City and Rex and Sally Lou. One of them is very mad and chain smoking cigarettes, imagining herself pummeling both TV hosts, the other is picturing herself in a courtroom, testifying on behalf of her friend in a lawsuit against the TV hosts, their producer, the network, and the mapmaker. She pictures herself in the witness box, raising her right hand and being sworn in and answering very cooly but pointedly the accusing questions of the defense attorney and utterly confounding him.

And shifting our gaze to the northern edge of the county, near a house off County Road X15, we see two FBI agents crammed inside a dugout filled with surveillance devices, biting their lips while they wait for help, hoping it arrives before the Remos storm outside. Behind them a ribbon of vans and cars with microwave antennas line one side of the road, with a cluster of cameramen and reporters facing the house at the entrance to the drive. Inside the house a very sick and exhausted woman lies on a sofa with her husband at her side, looking at fourteen charismatic Christians kneeling and praying for a vision from the Lord.

2.

As the Montana Militia roared down the highway towards Moosehead, the county seat of Rosebud County, they scanned the road front and back for cops. The boys kept their spirits stoked with plenty of Jim Beam and beer and big talk. With CBs in every car and pickup, they could plan their moves in concert. Thanks to a police scanner, they knew the deputies were on their way to the Randall Place for a standoff with a group holding a man and woman hostage. To handle the police, the militia had stopped at Alfred's house off Highway 25 and phoned in a call saying there was trouble at Bouncer's place in the northern part of the county, that they had heard gunshots and seen three trucks outside the house. Then they blackened their faces with charcoal from Alfred's barbecue grill and jumped back in their vehicles and pushed the accelerators to the floor.

It was precisely four-thirty Mountain Standard Time when the Montana Militia roared into Moosehead city limits. Moosehead was a dying town and business was slow on Friday evening. Aside from two dozen cars and pickups in front of Sidewinders and the other bars, the town was deserted.

"All right, boys," Cap crowed, "this town's wide open!"

"Yaaaahhooooo!"

"Whooeeee!"

"We go in, we get Lew, and that's it! No shooting! No rough stuff!"

They pulled up in front of the city hall and jumped out.

"No rifles," Cap said.

"No rifles?" Bouncer asked.

"You wanna be spotted?" Cap hissed.

The men threw their rifles in their cars and trucks.

"And hide the pistols, fer crissake!"

They stuck them in their pockets.

"Now let's move fast!" Cap said, and the fourteen men fought and pushed and shoved each other, squeezing through the station door.

Stacy, seeing this group of men with blackened faces push through the door, stood up.

"Sit down, sister!" Cap yelled, and she did. "Give me the keys to the jail!"

"I don't—I don't—I don't—"

"You don't what?! GET 'EM!! Give me the keys!!"

Cap drew his gun. Stacy's mouth dropped open, she pointed to the inside room.

"All right, up! Up! Up! Get up!"

Stacy stood.

"Get those keys!!!"

Trembling, weak in the knees, Stacy lurched towards the inside room, Sheriff Brandt's office. She opened his desk, pulled out a ring of keys and began fumbling.

"Hurry!" Cap whispered menacingly.

Stacy found the key and handed it to Cap. She looked into his eyes. He turned abruptly, telling Buck, "Keep an eye on her."

Then, followed by the others, he strode to the cells. Lew Mitchell was standing in the back cell, hands on bars, head pressed against them. He saw his friends.

"Hey, buddies!"

"Hey, Lew!" someone shouted.

"Damn, it's good to see you," Lew said, shaking his head in disbelief.

"We ain't gonna let a good buddy rot in a stinkin' government cell," Cap said, thrusting the key into the lock and turning it.

Lew pushed the door open and the men ran to the front room.

"Hey!" shouted Buck, "we better do sumthin' about this radio."

"Shit, yes," said Sonny, and the men began tearing out the phone, ripping out the cords, smashing the dials.

Then they were outside, laughing and joking, and they were still laughing as they sped out of town.

3.

Kline and Harris waited anxiously for the arrival of the ambulance and the sheriff's deputies. Harris had tied a tourniquet around Kline's ankle. The pain had set in, and Kline was grinding his teeth. "Where the hell is the sheriff? Where the hell is he?" he hissed.

At that moment Sheriff Brandt was sitting in his car, staring at a sign that said, "Bridge closed." Instead of driving down County Road R2T, he had driven the shortest way, thirty miles down gravel roads, and now this. He got out and walked to the bridge, which crossed a narrow stream. What if he tried crossing the stream in his car? Probably shallow enough. What about the embankment? It was somewhat steep and rugged, strewn with large rocks that could knock out his oil pan or transmission, or both. Did he dare chance it? Or should he take an alternate route that might take another thirty minutes? Thirty minutes could mean trouble for the hostages, the difference between life and death. He would have to chance crossing.

He located the best place for it, kicked a few rocks out of the way, got back in his car and slowly eased it off the road and towards the stream. Slowly, slowly, slowly. The front right wheel went over a rock and lifted the car up, then the body went down. Then went over another rock, tilted up on the left, went down. Bounce. Bump. Bump. Up high over another rock, down and smash on the underside. He was angling into the stream, and the car was on a slant. He hit another rock, went up and down. The car scraped: the hard scrape of rock against metal. He braked and thought. If he moved fast he could rip something out. But this was a crisis! Why was he waiting? What did a car matter compared to the lives of two people? He brought his foot down hard on the accelerator and the car moved only slightly as he heard something tear. Then he was stuck. He gunned the engine. The car roared in place.

He picked up his radio. "Five-two and five-three, this is five-one."

"I read you, sheriff," said one voice.

"Yeah, sheriff?" said another.

"I'm down on County Road R4X near the bridge," Brandt said. "My car's hung up, can't move."

"What happened?"

"Tried crossing on the bank, got hung up."

Five-two and five-three decided five-two was closest.

"I'm comin ta get ya, sheriff," said Deputy Holman, wondering why the sheriff tried crossing the bank. Was Brandt back on one of his toots?

Unknown to Sheriff Brandt and his deputies, their conversation was overheard by Cap as he and his friends rorared away from Moosehead. When he heard Bramdt, Cap called his buddies on the CB.

"Boys," said Cap, "I know just where ole Brandt is. Let's go find us a sheriff!" Cap, who was traveling at 75, lowered his foot on the pedal and moved the car up to 90. "I think we can beat that other ole boy."

Ten minutes later the Montana Militia was driving down County Road R4X and looking at the "Bridge Closed" sign on the bridge a hundred yards ahead. They slowed to a stop before the bridge and leaped out, guns in hand. Sheriff Brandt's car was stuck, with Brandt sitting in it. The sun was beginning to set.

The sheriff looked up into the barrels of a dozen guns held by men with blackened faces. He thought he recognized a few.

"Okay, sheriff," said Cap, "Out of the car."

Slowly, cautiously, Sheriff Brandt stepped out and stuck his hands in the air.

"What do you boys want?" he asked nervously.

"Nothin' much now, 'cept your gun. Don't you get it. We will. Sonny."

Sonny stepped forward and pulled the gun from Brandt's holster.

"Now boys," said Cap, "has anyone got some tools with 'em?"

"Like what?"

"Hammer, crowbar, socket wrench."

"Yeah," said Terry Heim.

"Terry, you get that stuff out of your car. Buck and Alfred, you take those tools and start tearin' down that sign. The rest of you hide your cars over there behind those bushes."

The men did as they were told. In five minutes the cars and men were hidden and the sign was down. A minute later they saw a car racing towards them.

Cap was afraid the deputy might slow to a stop when he saw the bridge and he did, but just for a moment. Then resumed speed. Cap and the boys were laughing and cheering as five-two, racing across the bridge, fell through the rotted boards and hung in mid-air, suspended by girders.

4.

Seconds after Stacy heard Cap, Byron, and the rest of the Montana Militia slam shut their pickup doors and roar out of town, she flew out the office and down the street towards the fire station, which also had a radio. Halfway to the fire station Stacey realized that the fire department, which was staffed entirely by volunteers, would be locked.

She had to get people on the roads looking for the town cop or Brandt or his deputies. The best place to go would be Sidewinders and maybe some of the other bars and get some of the boys looking.

Pickups were parallel parked up and down both sides of the street, outside the half dozen taverns on Main Street's two blocks. As she neared Sidewinders she could hear the beating of drums and the scream of loud guitars and a woman's loud whiney voice. When she opened the door, the blaring music and the smell of booze and a vaporous cloud of smoke and the shouting hit her at the same time. Even though it was only five o'clock, Sidewinders was packed. It was Friday and the denizens of Moosehead liked to get an early start on the weekend. The tables were full and the bar was lined with men and women wearing cowboy hats. To the right of the entry, Buster Butts' opening act, Dottie Lee Dills, sang on the low stage as a few couples, locked in death grips, made small steps on a tiny dance floor. In back, figures surrounded three pool tables.

Stacy knew it would be futile to try shouting over the noise. The only way to be heard was to get the microphone. She walked up to the stage and gestured to Dottie Lee, who ignored her. Finally Stacy stepped up on stage and began yelling.

The bouncer, "Red" Heck, emerged from the crowd and took her arm and called, "Get off 'a there," but Stacy ignored him and grabbed the microphone and began yelling into it: "Listen to me! Listen to me!"

The band stopped playing and Dottie Lee grabbed one of Stacy's arms while Red kept a grip on the other.

"Stop it! Stop it! Stop it!!" Stacy yelled at both of them.

Couples were laughing and pointing at her.

"Give me the microphone!" Dottie Lee yelled.

"The town is under attack!" Stacy screeched.

"She's drunk!" someone shouted.

"Throw her ass in the street!" someone else suggested.

As Red pulled her off the stage, Stacy dropped the microphone, which made a loud clanking noise.

"Shit, you damn bitch, you ruined my new microphone!" Dottie Lee yelled as Red pushed Stacy outside. "You'll pay for this! I'll kick your damn butt myself!"

Outside, Red told her, "You better get outa here before someone calls the cops."

"They can't call the cops! That's what I wanted to say!"

"You're lucky someone didn't bust your butt."

"Listen to me. I'm the police dispatcher. I came here for help. Some people just came to the sheriff's office and smashed up the radio."

"You bet," Red said.

Just then a woman stepped outside the bar. "Stacy," she asked, "what's up?"

"Cora," Stacy said, recognizing the woman, "a group of men with blackened faces busted into the office, took the prisoner, and smashed the radio. That's what I was tryin' to tell people."

"You ain't drunk?"

"No, I'm not drunk."

"You know her?" Red asked Cora.

"Hell, yes, this is Stacy Miles. She's Brandt's dispatcher."

"And there's no way of tellin' Arlan what's happened," Stacy said. "There's no other dispatch radio in town."

"You say they took a prisoner?" Red asked.

"Yeah. Lew Mitchell. That's what they come for."

"All right, let's get this news out," Red said and walked back inside, followed by the two women.

Dottie Lee was explaining to the audience: "I never had nothin' like that happen an' I been singin' thirteen years. I've dealt with all kinds of drunks, believe me, but nothin' like that one."

As Red approached Dottie, she looked in his direction and saw Stacy. She was about to say something when Red told her, "She came here with a message for the town."

"I got a message for her," Dottie Lee barked. "If she don't get her damn ass outa here, I'm gonna plug it with a baseball bat."

Red threw up his arms and called, "Listen, everyone. There's a gang in town that broke into the sheriff's office an' tore it up. They busted out a prisoner and smashed up the dispatch radio."

Several men stood up.

"What the hell—!"

"How you know that?"

"Where are they?"

More and more people were crowding around.

"This woman," Red announced, pointing to Stacy, "is Sheriff Brandt's dispatcher. That's what she came to tell us."

"Who were they?" someone asked Stacy.

"Their faces was all blackened. I didn't recognize none of 'em."

"How many were there?" someone else asked.

"A couple dozen."

"Hell, what we waitin' for? Let's get lookin' for 'em," a man said and made for the door.

The others followed and Sidewinder's clientele emptied onto the sidewalk.

5.

Lorene and Jeannie had just settled into their seats when the plane's turbines turned over with a roar. The two ladies looked at each other and grinned broadly.

"Hot damn!" said Lorene.

"Double hot damn!" Jeannie replied.

"We're gonna have us a good time and fix the dirty butts of those two New York smarty pants."

"You're damn straight we'll fix their pants. Say, we need a drink. We should be toastin' this trip." Jeannie leaned into the aisle, saw the stewardess and called, "Waitress!"

The stewardess saw her and said, "Just a minute, please." She went to the front of the cabin and told everyone to buckle up.

"We shoulda brought our own booze," Jeannie said.

"I wasn't thinkin'," Lorene said.

"You had a lot on your mind, what with bein' flimflammed an' all."

"Yer right."

"I've half a mind to get up and mix my own drink," Jeannie said.

The two ladies had bought a six-pack for the drive to Billings and had finished it by the time they arrived at the airport. They even had enough time before their flight to have a drink at the bar.

"I've half a mind to help you mix 'em," Lorene said.

"Didn't you bring a flask?"

"No."

"What has come over you? This is not the Lorene Simpson I used to know."

"I had a lot on my mind today, what with bein' flimflammed an' all."

"You coulda thought about it. I don't think in your situation you can afford to be makin' excuses for yerself. That is definitely not goin' to help the situation. You are going to have to stay clearheaded with all that we've gotta do the next two days. So don't you start feelin sorry for yourself."

"I am NOT feelin' sorry for myself."

"The hell yer not. That's all yer thinkin about is yer troubles. That's why you forgot to bring a flask. We're outa booze cuza you."

"You coulda brought some!"

Passengers were starting to look at the two women, but their argument was drowned in the roar of engines as the plane surged forward and lifted off the ground. Soon the stewardesses were pushing trays with drinks down the aisle.

"I'm sorry now I even came on this trip," Jeannie said.

"I didn't ask you to come."

"The hell you didn't. Why the hell do you think I'm here?"

"You asked to go!"

"Bullshit!"

"Bullshit yourself," Lorene shot back. "I know what you said. You said you wanted to come to give me moral support."

"Yeah, when you was actin' like a friend." Pause. "Not now you ain't."

"Ain't what?"

"Ain't actin' like a friend," Jeannie said. "Without me you won't do nothin'."

"Watch me."

"I've got better things to do," Jeannie announced. "I'm gonna go out to dinner an' see a show. "

"If you think I'm payin' for your trip after this yer crazy."

"You just better stop talkin' right now. Yer sinking lower

and lower."

"You are nasty. An' now that yer talkin' nasty you can bet I won't pay for it."

"You never did offer to pay for it."

The stewardess with the tray was now alongside.

"And what would you like?" she asked Jeannie sweetly.

"A double bourbon."

"And you?" she asked Lorene.

"Seven an' Seven."

She gave the ladies their drinks and moved on.

Jeannie took a big swallow. "So yer not payin' me back for my fare."

"Nope. Why should I?"

"You said you were."

"The hell . . ."

They both took another drink.

Jeannie said, "I'm sorry I ever came on this trip."

"I'm sorry you came too."

"I shoulda stayed home an' made Bouncer a nice dinner."

"Huh!" Lorene grunted.

"What's that supposed to mean?"

"Dinner? You cook Bouncer dinner? Don't make me laugh."

"I cook dinner almost every night."

"Yeah, what? Fried beans an' hot dawgs?"

"I should throw this drink right in yer face."

"Try it!" Lorene held her own drink up, ready to throw it at her friend.

"I got better things to do than to waste good booze on you. I'm gonna have it myself," Jeannie said and finished her drink.

"I got better things to do with my drink too!" Lorene said, and finished off her own.

"Now I'm gonna have a nap, and don't bother me," Jeannie said.

"Don't you bother me!" Lorene said, and snuggled into her seat with her head on a pillow, propped between the wall and seat.

"I have no intention to," Jeannie said, and lowered her seat and laid back.

Both went to sleep. Within minutes, Lorene was snoring loudly. They slept until they landed in Minneapolis, when Jeannie woke and nudged Lorene.

"Huh?" Lorene said and looked at Jeannie.

"Hello," Jeannie said.

"You talkin' to me?"

"Yeah, I'm talkin' to you. We're on a trip, we should be enjoyin' ourselves. We got us a vacation, let's act like it's one."

Lorene said, "I agree."

"You sorry for what you said to me?"

"If you're sorry for what you said."

"I'm sorry if you're sorry." Jeannie paused. "Yer right. We don't gotta do dishes for two days, we don't gotta clean house, we don't gotta listen to a lot of bull roar."

"Isn't it awful to be fightin' with yer best friend?" Lorene said.

"It sure as hell is. You are my best friend."

"Well, you're mine."

6.

Inside the Remos' house, Reverend Enoch Angle knelt on the floor, praying out loud, surrounded by his kneeling followers. Mr. and Mrs. Travers sat on the floor, away from windows.

"Listen, now, listen," Angle adjured his people.

The voices grew quieter.

"Listen."

All were silent.

"The Lord has silenced the forces of the Anti-Christ."

They listened.

"Not a sound."

"That's right," Charles Dinkins said.

"Let us listen for the Lord's direction."

They were silent again, during which time Mr. Travers leaned over to his wife and whispered, "We've got to get away."

"What happened out there?" Mrs. Travers whispered back.

"You had an asthma attack. They brought you in. Two crazy men out there started shooting." While he talked with her, Mr. Travers kept his eyes on the Remos.

"Who was shooting?" she whispered, thinking it was the Remos.

"I don't know. Crazy men. They're still outside, I think."

She looked even more distraught. "Who are these people?"

"I don't know."

"A gang?"

"I don't know."

"They must be if someone's trying to kill them."

"We've got to get away."

"Not if those others are still outside."

"I know."

"I'm not going out there," she told him.

"Well, I don't know what to do."

"Tell me about it." She looked at him hard, and said, "Nothing changes."

7.

Immediately after returning to his condominium that afternoon Rex had looked at his 1956 U.S. atlas and looked at the continental map. There was Montana. How could Jelton's plan work? The blood rushed to his head and the veins in the back of his skull begin to pulse. He could see the tabloid headlines: "REX'S SECRET SHAME: I FLUNKED FIRST GRADE!" and "'MONTANA?' ASKS REX, 'WHO'S THAT?'"

Making matters worse, Jelton had been insulting viewers who called to complain. And, of course, Sally Lou didn't know any better. Well, not exactly. She, at least, suspected that Montana might be a state. But so had he. He had told that Rates woman he thought the map was "a piece of shhh—" when Sally Lou had cut him off. Of course he knew Montana was a state. But as far as the press and public were concerned that didn't matter. They'd all look stupid. Everyone would be all over them.

Not just the tabloids, but *People*, the entertainment weeklies, the dailies, even the *New York Times*. Viewers wouldn't respect them anymore. They'd lose ratings. He lose the show!

If they could only somehow get through the next few days, then the inevitable hoopla would die down and their gaff would be forgotten. But could they get through the next few days? Well, he told himself, there is no such thing as bad publicity. If everyone thought he was a fool, they'd tune in just to see how big a fool he was. Yes! This would work in his favor. No need to get upset. Just cool down.

He had discussed the problem with his wife, Judy, and she agreed that the publicity could only help. Then they began getting calls from acquaintances who kidded them about the screwup. After a few of these calls they let the answering machine take messages.

Rex told Judy about Wellstone's party and wondered if they should go. Wellstone never had impromptu parties, nor did anyone else they knew. Dickie had seen him at lunch and, having seen the show that morning, no doubt had decided to have some fun that evening at their expense. Still, he would go. Wellstone was extremely well-connected within the industry and more than one person worth schmoozing with would be there. In addition to holding onto the current show, Rex very much wanted to host a new evening show—a celebrity show that combined wrestling with a ten-question quiz—that was scheduled to open in five months. Two of Wellstone's friends had bought the rights, and just might be there.

Judy stood in front of their hall mirror, adjusting her straw hat as Rex looked over her shoulder.

"You look terrific, babe," he said, regarding his own image in the mirror.

"So do you."

She turned and adjusted his tie quickly.

"All right, let's do it," she said.

His face reflected his ambivalence about the party.

"What's the matter?" she asked.

"I don't know, just a feeling that tonight is a setup."

"For what?"

"Jokes, at my expense. They're going to be all over me."

"Well, you should've known Montana's a state."

"Should have known, should have known," Rex snapped. "That helps a lot."

"Cool down."

"The whole industry is going to know it."

"Tell them you thought it was a joke and you went along with it."

"Jelton had the same idea. Tomorrow I'm to announce that we thought that map was a gag. I'll say that of course we know Montana is a state, only an idiot wouldn't! That's why I played it to the hilt."

"Exactly. You better get a hold of Sally Lou and get her to tell the same story."

"She knows."

"Remind her now so she doesn't screw up at Wellstone's."

Rex walked to the phone stand and dialed. No answer. He tried her cell phone. No answer.

"Shit. She and the moron are probably on their way over to Wellstone's right now."

"Corner her over there. Stop worrying about it."

Rex felt a tremendous burden lifted from him. But after their doorman hailed a cab and they climbed inside, the despair returned.

"What about that woman from Montana, the one I screamed at? We can't explain her away as a gag. We picked her name from a bunch of slips."

"Grand Tally managed to stuff the bowl. Her name was on all the slips. She happens to be a New York actress hired for the gag."

Rex thought about that. "That won't work. Grand Tally wouldn't hire an actress to draw attention to their fuckup. On national T.V.?"

"You tell them you thought the woman was an actress. You thought it was a publicity ploy."

"That's right! That'll work! And I didn't think it was a joke until I looked at that screwed up map—which was so ridiculous—when I saw that then I figured this had to be a setup, complete with an actress impersonating a Montana hillbilly! So I pretended I didn't think Montana was a state." Rex paused. "We ought to sue Grand Tally for causing us all this anguish and embarrassment."

"Yeah," Judy said, turning to Rex. "Why *not* threaten them?"

"Perfect!"

Rex reached in his inside jacket pocket, pulled out his cell phone, and dialed Jelton's number.

"Jelton's gonna love this!" Rex beamed.

Jelton answered the phone. "Hello?"

"Jelton! I have the answer!"

"To what?"

It was clear from his tone that Jelton was depressed.

"To the Montana problem."

"We solved that problem this morning."

"No we didn't. Did you see the evening news?" Rex asked. "You know that shootout in Montana?"

"Are you on drugs?"

"Whaddaya mean?"

"We're having relatives of the crazies on tomorrow, fer crissake."

"I know! But do you know where the shootout is?"

"Montana."

"Moosehead, Montana!"

"So?"

"That's where that woman called from!"

"Oh, shit," Jelton groaned.

"But I'll say that that map was such an obvious piece of shit that we figured they were putting us on. That I figured the woman who answered the phone was an actress hired by Grand Tally. That's why I got so rude with her! I figured that whole deal was a publicity ploy by Grand Tally to promote the map."

"Pretty fuckin' stupid publicity ploy."

"It doesn't matter!!!!!!! The point is, I thought it was."

Jelton brightened. “I like that.”

“Good idea, huh? I’m full of them. Here’s one that’s even better—we announce we’re gonna sue Grand Tally for setting us up like that.”

“Sue ‘em for that? That’s ridiculous.”

“We don’t have to go through with it. Just threaten them. It makes us look good. We get completely off the hook, they come off looking like wet butt holes.”

“I like that. Good man.”

Judy was looking at Rex all the while. “Tell him whose idea it was,” she said.

Rex waved her off.

She grabbed the phone and said into it, “It was my idea.”

“Who’re you?” Jelton wanted to know.

“Judy,” she said. “It was my idea.”

“Figures,” Jelton said. “Tell Rex he’s still an asshole.”

CHAPTER SEVEN

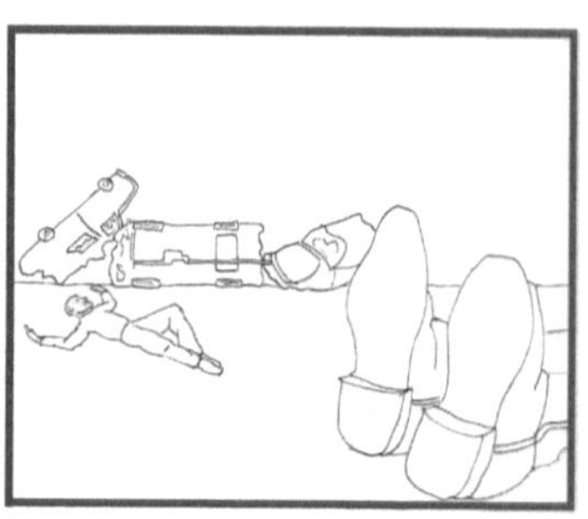

As Deputy Sheriff Holman climbed out of his car onto the collapsed planks of the bridge, the Montana militia stood waiting for him with guns levelled.

Brandt said nothing as Holman edged carefully towards the men standing at the foot of the bridge. Now that the shock was over, Holman could barely keep his knees from buckling. "Who are you?" he wanted to know.

"Shut up, deputy," Buck drawled.

As Holman stepped off the bridge, someone asked, "What're we gonna do with 'em?"

"What's up?" Holman asked weakly.

"We're gonna cuff ya," Cap said.

Brandt and Holman's hands were pulled behind their backs. Buck and Sonny took the handcuffs from the officers belts and snapped them on the lawmen's wrists.

Brandt was too scared to speak but Holman was too scared to stop talking. "What're you gonna do with us?" he wanted to know.

"You talk too much," Cap hissed and put a six-shooter to the deputy's head and cocked the hammer.

Holman quivered.

"Someone," Cap ordered, "smash up Brandt's radio."

Alfred took his rifle and began smashing Brandt's dashboard with the gunstock. Then he ripped out the radio speaker and cord. Finally, for good measure, he fired a few rounds into the instrument panel.

"Shoot Brandt's tires," someone suggested, and Alfred obliged, putting a bullet into each. Buck did the same for Holmen's car.

"Who's got rope?" Cap asked.

"I do," Bouncer offered.

"Get it," Cap ordered.

Minutes later Brandt and Holman lay on the ground with their ankles bound and a rope tying their ankles to their handcuffs.

"Ahhhh," Holman moaned, "this hurts."

"Ah, isn't that a shame," Cap clucked. "Wittle deputy's ankles hurt. My, my."

"No, it's my wrists."

"Isn't that too fuckin' bad!" roared Sonny. "Mebbe you shoulda thought 'a that before you took this job!"

"You ain't got no authority," Buck told the lawmen between clenched teeth.

"Your days of ridin' roughshod over this county is over," someone else said.

"Should I put a bullet in their damn heads?" Sonny asked Cap.

"No," Cap replied, "we're gonna leave 'em here. With the bridge out, it may be a while before anyone finds 'em. And by then mebbe the vultures will've picked 'em over."

Everybody laughed.

"Let's head for that shootout with those FBI boys," Cap shouted and the men raced for their cars.

2.

Outside Sidewinder's, the fear and fury of the mob began growing.

"Let's get this thing organized," said Red.

"Organize, hell, Red. What's to organize? Just about everyone's got a CB. Let's just get in our damn pickups an' drive like hell. Anywhere. Everywhere. I'm through talkin'." With that the speaker, still grasping his beer bottle, dashed across the street to his pickup and drove off.

Five or six others, seeing their friend leave town, gave a

shout and ran for their own trucks.

Red, his hands raised, addressed the rest. "The people we're after are armed. So let's go in pairs. Two to a vehicle. If you run into them, don't do nothin' on your own. Get on the radio and inform the others."

A tall woman in snakeskin boots, tight jeans and black stetson said, "I ain't gonna wait fer no backup. Bobby"—the man standing next to her—"and me's got a shotgun. I kin do a hellova lot of damage with that baby. You all kin mop up what Bobby an' me don't finish off."

"Now Brenda, that's just the kind of thinking that'll get us hurt," Red advised the group.

"Red," said Brenda, "you always was a candy ass. Bobby, let's roll."

Brenda turned on her heel and began striding off, followed by her boyfriend.

"Yeah, we all got a rifle or a shotgun," someone else offered. "I don't see the danger."

"Listen," Red said, raising his voice, "let's figure where we're all gonna go so we're not all coverin' the same ground. Who'll take Highway 38 an' the roads in the northwest sector of the county?"

Three hands shot up.

"All right. You boys go."

They took off.

"Now who'll cover the northeast sector between Griner's Corners, Big Hat, and Bad Medicine?"

Four hands shot up.

"All right, boys, take off."

And so Red continued until the last of the crowd dispersed. Then he made the rounds of the other bars. By six-thirty he had over 150 volunteers roaring up and down Rosebud County roads, searching for the men who had broken into the Moosehead jail.

3.

It was dark by the time an ambulance came screaming up to the

Randall Place. From their windows the Remos saw the ambulance arrive, its lights flashing and siren wailing.

Harris crawled out of the dugout, yelling, "DAMMIT!" and waving his arms as he ran towards the vehicles.

The ambulance driver and paramedic jumped out and ran towards him.

"Where's the victim?"

"Turn those lights off! Turn off the lights!"

"What's up, chief?"

"Turn off your lights!"

The driver turned them off.

"Follow me," Harris said, and led the paramedics to the dugout where they carefully lifted Kline.

"Big toe got shot off?" the paramedic asked.

"Yeah," said Harris.

"Is it bleeding, pal?" the paramedic asked Kline.

"Not now," Kline said.

As they began carrying Kline up the slope, a sheriff's deputy arrived with police lights flashing and siren wailing. He took his time getting out of his car, as though responding to a stolen vehicle report. His lights were still flashing as he got his papers together.

"Turn off the lights!" Harris hollered at him.

Deputy Schmidt emerged slowly from the car. "What's the problem here?"

"You are! Turn those lights off! We got a hostage situation. Turn off the fuckin' lights."

Deputy Schmidt swung back into the car and turned them off.

At the end of the drive, twenty feet away, cameras taped the scene.

The paramedics now had Kline inside the ambulance and were examining his foot.

Harris asked the deputy, "You got a bull horn?"

"In the trunk."

"Get it."

Schmidt waddled to the back of his car and fetched the

speaker.

Harris switched it on and faced the Remos' house. "This is the FBI. You are surrounded. Come out with a white flag and your hands up."

Harris and the deputy watched the house.

"How many're in there?" Schmidt asked.

"Ten or twelve. They got two hostages."

"Who are the hell are they?"

"Cultists. Crazies. They shot my partner. If anyone steps outside without a white flag—man or woman—shoot to kill." He turned to Schmidt. "Got that deputy?"

"Yeah," Schmidt said, not sure that he would shoot. "You say they got hostages?"

"Yeah, they got hostages. A man and a woman."

"How'd this happen?"

"Whaddaya mean, 'How'd this happen?' How do you think hostages get taken?"

"I mean . . . why?"

"Just watch the door," Harris said and walked off.

"Okay," Schmidt called after him but returned to his car and called into his radio. "This is Unit five-three. Units five-one, five-two, respond."

No answer.

"Units five-one and five-two, please respond. We have a hostage situation at the Randall place. FBI requests backup."

Three miles away and back in their cars, the Moosehead contingent of the Montana militia was listening to Deputy Schmidt over the police scanner and cackling. "Boys," said Cap over the CB to the men in the other vehicles, "this is it. We're gonna make history. It's freedom at stake. Let's get 'em good." And he gunned his car for the Randall place.

4.

At that moment millions of people across the country were watching a CDC network sitcom. Suddenly it was interrupted with a picture of the CDC News logo and a voice saying: "We interrupt this program to bring you a special news bulletin" and the camera cut to David Whortley saying: "A violent episode unfolds this evening in rural Montana, where a group of evangelical Christian cultists are holding two hostages inside their heavily guarded compound. All that stands between the cultists and the possible destruction of the nearby town of Moosehead are two law officers waiting against hope for a peaceful resolution to this crisis. Standing by is CDC corespondent-at-large, Gus Harvey, with the latest information. Good evening, Gus."

The screen filled with the image of Gus Harvey, standing fifty yards in front of the Remos' house.

GUS: Good evening, David.

DAVID: Gus, what is the latest in this tragedy?

GUS: Everyone here is waiting for what may develop into one of the bloodiest episodes in recent American history. Since one FBI agent was shot this morning, we have only the unconfirmed rumor of another shooting, that of a Montana deputy sheriff. I must underline 'unconfirmed.' The FBI are not allowing us access beyond this area."

(Harvey gestured towards the woods and house.)

GUS: Our only sources are the few citizens who have ventured here. The federal police and local sheriff's department are keeping mum.

DAVID: Gus, have the Remos made any demands?

GUS: No, David, they haven't. This is all very mysterious. Why would they take hostages when they are expecting the Second Coming?

DAVID: You've been covering the Remos for the last five days, what can you tell us about their psychological profile?

GUS: Well, the experts are divided. Some psychiatrists speculate that when Christ does not reappear the group will commit mass suicide. Others believe that they may take their disappointment out on others, with bloody results. We can only hope that a hostage negotiator arrives in time to resolve this ugly situation.

DAVID: Do you have any word on a negotiator?

GUS: None. As I said, the FBI and sheriff's department are

running a closed operation.

DAVID: What is the name of the wounded FBI agent, and how badly is he hurt?

GUS: The FBI won't tell us his name, but it appears that his right foot and knee cap have sustained serious injury. He was unable to walk. In fact, minutes ago two paramedics carried him to an ambulance.

DAVID: Have the agents received any backup from other law enforcement agencies?

GUS: Only one deputy sheriff, David, and that's been one of the big surprises. Everyone is asking, Where are the sheriff and the other deputies? The deputy here has no information on that.

DAVID: That's incredible.

GUS: Yes, it is, David. We have no idea of exactly how many weapons the Remos have or if and when they may emerge from their compound. Obviously if they chose to attack the two lawmen, they could easily overpower them. I have to say that these lawmen have shown extreme bravery in holding their position. And frankly, I'm getting a little worried for their safety and even for our own.

DAVID: I want to remind our viewers, and tell those who just tuned in, that an evangelical Christian cult, the Remos, launched an unprovoked attack on two FBI agents at the cult's hideout in Moosehead, Montana. Gus, has anyone heard anything from the Remos? Or seen them?

GUS: No, David. We've not seen the Remos since they barricaded themselves inside their compound. We don't know the condition of the hostages.

DAVID: Isn't it unusual that this standoff has been in progress for two hours and the FBI has not sent reinforcements?

GUS: You can be sure that reinforcements are on the way. Bear in mind that Moosehead is a long way from the nearest airport, so any help is going to be a long time in coming.

DAVID: Tell us, if you will, how many cult members are in the fortress, and whether there are any children inside.

GUS: There are twenty-one inside the compound. Five

adult couples and six children.

DAVID: This could have some very unfortunate consequences.

GUS: It certainly could, and everyone here is praying that the children and the hostages are released before there is any more violence.

DAVID: What are the chances of a peaceful resolution?

GUS: Unfortunately, the chances appear slim.

DAVID: Well, let us hope and pray that this situation doesn't end in a burst of bombs or gunfire. Thank you, Gus, for keeping us posted.

Gus disappeared from the screen.

DAVID: We now resume our regular broadcast. Stay tuned to CDC for the latest developments in Moosehead, Montana.

5.

While Moosehead's self-appointed posse scattered in all directions, Alicia Clapper and Thornton Granger were busy at their midtown Manhattan office, planning Grand Tally's comprehensive offensive strategy.

At this moment the pair were hammering out a press release to send every major news outlet, including Reuters, the BBC, and Al Jezera.

While Clapper sat behind a wide mahogany desk making notes on her laptop, Granger paced the floor, throwing out ideas.

"As we told Feinstein and whatisname," Granger said, "the fault lies with the printer. What was the name of that printer?"

Clapper lifted a yellow pad and turned back several pages. "Hughes Brothers."

"The Chicago firm? The big gun?"

"Yes."

"Piece of cake," said Granger, and laughed. "The internationally known Hughes Brothers is about to get a very bloody nose."

Clapper raised her eyebrows.

Granger continued. "The *Wall Street Journal* just ran a story on Hughes. The Asian competition has them on their last legs. They're tottering on the precipice. A major lawsuit, or the threat of one, could push them over the edge." Granger rubbed his hands together. "All right, let's start writing."

An hour later Granger called Feinstein and read him the press release.

"You two are the best," Feinstein admitted. "Run with it."

6.

With only an hour left of their flight to New York, Lorene and Jeannie were planning the next day's events.

Lorene was thinking out loud. "We gotta find out where they hold that crooked show, "Rex and Sally Lou."

"CDC studios, I expect," said Jeannie.

"For all we know they have four or five studios."

"Well, we'll just call CDC."

"I wonder if you have to have an appointment to get in the audience."

"A reservation like?"

"Yeah," Lorene said. "I been thinkin' about that an' it bothers me. What if you have to have a reservation and the place is full up?"

"Reckon we could sneak through."

"What if they got guards?"

"Bribe 'em. I think twenty bucks would speak as loud as a megaphone."

"May-be. What if it don't?"

"Then we'll wait for the two chiselers and clean their clocks outside."

"Sounds like a plan," said Lorene and settled back in her seat. In her mind she imagined Jeannie and herself standing at a side entrance to the studio. When the side door opens, Rex and Sally Lou walk out and Lorene steps in front of the squirrely little man.

"Recognize my voice?" she asks.

"No," Rex says, smiling.

"You don't?" she purrs. "Oh, come on, Rex, think. Yesterday's drawing? Moosehead, Montana, the state that doesn't exist? You remember that."

The expression on Rex's face quickly switches from pleasure to annoyance.

"I don't have time to talk about that," Rex says and tries to walk around her, but Lorene steps in his way.

"I'm Lorene Simpson, the woman you called a liar—on national television!"

'I'm sorry. Did I call you a liar? I don't think so," he replies with a touch of disdain.

Lorene gives him a fast, sharp push in the chest.

"Stop!!!!" screams Sally Lou.

At that Jeannie (standing beside Lorene), yells into Sally Lou's ear: "SHUTTT UPPPPP!!!!" and shoves her into Rex.

When Rex tries to fight back the two women attack them with fists flying. The two New Yorkers take off running across 45th Street in midtown traffic, screaming for help.

7.

Buck was sitting shotgun in Cap's pickup as the Montana militia sped down a gravel road and onto Highway 25, toward town.

"What now, Cap? Where to?" Buck asked.

"We're gonna find us some FBI agents an' have us some fun!"

Buck took a pull on his pint of Jim Beam. "This has been one rockin' good night, Cap."

"You said it, buddy."

Buck passed the bottle to Cap, who put the hammer to the pedal.

As they hotrodded down the highway followed by their friends (all hooting and hollering), they came in sight of the Travers' car alongside the road.

"That car was there when we drove out," said Buck.

"Yup," Cap replied.

As they passed the car Buck glanced at the license plate illuminated in the highlights.

"Them are out of state plates, Cap."

"Yup."

"Slow down, Cap."

"Huh?"

"Slow down, I want to check that car."

The truck sped on.

"Cap, I got me a hunch that's my sister's car."

"Your sister?"

"Supposed to have arrived here on Thursday. Been missin' three days."

Cap slammed on the brakes, and the pickup slid sideways. No one behind had a chance to stop.

BAM! (Bouncer's pickup slammed into Cap's pickup, which spun 180 degrees.) BOOM! (Alfred's car rammed Bouncer's pickup.) RRRRKKKKKK!!! (Brice's car slammed into Alfred's car.) BOOM! (Alfred's car lurched forward hitting Bouncer's pickup and ricocheted backwards into Cap's pickup.) BAM! Bump! Bump! Bump! (Cap's pickup spun off the road and rolled sideways into the ditch and upside down.) As the last of the vehicles ceased moving, there was, for a moment, silence. Then came yowls and cries. "Ahhhh!!!" A dull groan. Someone swearing. Then a prolonged yell. A howl. Another dull groan. From each car and truck came the sounds of suffering.

Cap lay on the roof of the cab with his feet entangled in the steering column. As he regained consciousness, Cap heard Buck moan. He opened his eyes slowly and saw his friend's crumpled body lying amid shattered glass. For a moment he wondered what had happened. His head hurt. He heard the sounds from the other vehicles. He had to help his friends.

As the groans grew louder, Cap Matlock ever so slowly pulled his legs down to his chest and under the steering wheel. His window was open. But before he swung his legs outside, he tried to sense pain in his back or neck. No pain. Slowly, cautiously, he swung his legs out the window. He took his time standing. He was dazed, almost unable to believe what had happened. He looked about at the wrecked vehicles and listened to the moans of his injured friends. He could hear Buck stirring inside the cab.

Cap hobbled around to Buck's side. His friend was upside down and held by the seat belt. Cap leaned down and asked, "Buck, are you all right?"

"Get me outa here," Buck groaned.

"Anything feel broken?"

"I doan know. Jus' get me out."

Cap opened the door and fumbled for the buckle, then dragged his friend outside.

"Lay me out flat, Cap."

Cap stretched him out in the ditch beside the road as Bouncer emerged from his cab, crawling on hands and knees. Cap searched the different vehicles.

"No one's dead, thank God," he thought.

Pee Wee and Alfred were the only ones beside Bouncer and himself who were able to walk.

"Let's see if any of these vehicles is workin'," Cap said.

They discovered that Alfred's car and Bouncer's pickup would move, though with considerable screeching and scratching.

"Let's get everyone in the truck an' car," Cap said.

"Cap," Bouncer said, holding a severely bruised and cut arm, "the boys may be too busted up t'move. For all we know, one of 'em may have a busted neck. We might kill 'em if we move 'em."

"An' I'm thinking we got no choice. We cain't stay out here."

"Why the hell not?"

"'Cause with Brandt an' his deputies hogtied by the river, we just might end up doin' seventy years in the pen, that's why."

The four men began carrying the others to the back of Bouncer's pickup. It took them ten minutes to find the unconscious Byron Pulver lying in a clump of mesquite.

"Alfred," Cap said, "you drive Bouncer's car. Follow me."

"Where we goin'?" Alfred asked.

"Buck's."

With most of the men laid out on the bed of Bouncer's pickup, the two vehicles drove off, rattling and scraping as they made their way down the road, their front ends jerking back and forth from loosened tie rods, sounding like a hundred washers in an oil drum rolling down hill. Behind them lay the wrecks of two trucks and a car and a road strewn with shattered glass and metal.

CHAPTER EIGHT

As the sun began to fall behind the western mountain range, Sheriff Brandt and Deputy Holman were scooting on their backs across the hard-scrabble ground to Holman's car. Fifteen minutes earlier, Brandt had figured that if they could edge their way to the car, they might be able to saw through their ropes on the shattered fender.

Holman was cursing quietly as he inched his way across the dirt.

"These damn pebbles! They like to poke a hole in m'back. . . . Ouch!!!"

"I'm tired of listenin' to your whinin', Holman."

Brandt stoically pushed with his feet and scraped backwards three inches.

"Your back," Holman complained, "is not bein' poked with these stones an' sticks."

"You whiney little weasel," Brandt said. "The minute we get back to town you better start lookin' for another job."

Holman pushed with his feet and slid four inches towards the car. "Like I was plannin' on keepin' this one. Half the people in this damn county are psycho. When I get out of this mess"—he shoved with his feet—"I'm headed outa here."

Twenty minutes later the two lawmen were within a few feet of the car. Slowly and painfully Brandt rotated his body so his feet faced the wrecked vehicle. Holman, panting furiously, also managed to face it.

Brandt dug his feet in the ground and pulled himself forward a half a foot. He raised his legs as far as he could and placed the ropes over the metal. Then he began pulling and pushing his legs back and forth.

2.

"Reverend," said Charles "The Rock" Dinkins.

"Yes?" answered Reverend Angle.

The Remos' leader now sat on the floor, away from the windows, eating a ham sandwich. All the Remos sat away from windows.

"I've been wonderin' about these folks here," Dinkins said, nodding at the Traverses.

The Traverses were sitting in a corner by themselves. Mr. Travers was studying the floor and thinking, while Mrs. Travers was biting her lips.

Angle turned his head and looked. "What about them?"

"It don't seem right that they're here."

"Why? The Lord put 'em here."

"Can you be sure? Did the Lord speak to you about that?"

"No. Can't say he has."

"That's my point. The Lord's said nothing to you about them, and they're scared as can be."

Angle saw that Mrs. Travers was biting her lip and Mr. Travers was miles away. The Clingmeier daughters were sitting huddled with their mother, clearly frightened.

"It don't seem right that the children should be here, either."

Carl Clingmeier heard that. "The children got as much right as you!"

"Right?" Dinkins asked.

"When you get shot up by them madmen out there," Clingmeier said, " you know where you're goin'. Straight t' heaven. 'Cause that's God's plan. Same as'll happen to me and Greta when we get shot up. We're goin' t' heaven. Everyone here that gets shot up is goin' t' heaven. That's God's plan! So that's why the childrun is stayin'. I ain't robbin' them of their chance t' go to heaven RIGHT NOW! And you ain't either. The childrun stays!"

"Your little boy an' girl is scared t' death," Dinkins told Clingmeier.

"So what?! What's four, five, even ten hours of bein' scared t' death when their reward is an eternity in heaven? Tell me that!"

"I wanna go," whined the little Clingmeier girl.

"Me too," said the boy.

"See!" Carl cried. "They wanna go t' heaven!"

"No," the girl said in a trembling voice, "I want to leave."

"Not deep in yer heart yeh don't. Deep in yer heart yeh love Lord Jesus more'n anything else. Ain't that right?" Carl turned to Reverend Angle. "She's a good girl, a real Christian, praise Jesus."

"What's that supposed t' mean?" asked Dinkins. "That because she loves Jesus she ought t' be shot full of holes?"

While the two men argued, George Slow Bear was braiding his hair and softly humming a Lakota death chant. He had made up his mind to kill as many of the devils outside as he could, before they killed him. He had broken off the legs of a chair and whittled the ends to points. He knew he might not get the chance to use his simple weapons, but if any agent of the Anti-Christ broke through a door or window, he would plunge a stake into his heart.

While Slow Bear hummed and saw visions of his ancestors riding into battle, Jeb and Letta Hudson played guitar and hammered dulcimer together and sang an old Appalachian folk song, "Seein' Jesus at the Gates."

"I'm headed up to heaven
An' will see those pearly gates,
Oh I'm goin' up to heaven
To see Jesus at the gates."

Mrs. Clingmeier joined in on the second chorus.

"Seein' Jesus (seein' Jesus)
At them gates
Oh I'm goin' (yeah I'm goin')
To see Jesus (to see Jesus)
At them pearly
at them pearly
at them pearly, golden gates."

As they raised their voices in jubilation the other Remos clapped a beat and shouted affirmations. Reverend Angle got to his feet and began dancing, arms out, head thrown back, whirling in circles and shouting "Jesus! Jesus! I see Jesus at them pearly gates!" Even Slow Bear put away his sharpened sticks and tapped a foot to the beat.

Carl Clingmeier and the Dinkinses continued arguing. The children cried. Suddenly the rest of the Remos were shouting in tongues, "GLEBDERFERMEIT!! LOTTATANGDOMINQUE!! BASATANRAY ROY MINIMAL!!

3.

Outside in the dugout, agent Harris listened to the singing through his head phones. What the hell were these people singing for? he wondered. What did they have to sing about? Fuckin' idiots. And what was that shouting? Oh yeah, tongues.

He finally decided that crazy people will do anything. This was a cult and their song was part of a ritual. Maybe a death ritual. Who the hell knew. But he was sure of one thing: that the Remos were working themselves into a frenzy and there was only he and deputy Schmidt to stop them from rampaging out of the house.

"Schmidt!" he called to the deputy as he pulled off his head phones.

"Yeah?"

"Get ready. I think they're going to come crashin' out."

"I better get backup!" Schmidt was shaking. He wanted to drive off, but he said, "I'll try the sheriff."

"Call the sheriff, call the Moosehead police. Get someone!"

Harris and Schmidt left the dugout and positioned themselves behind the deputy's car. Harris clutched the AK-47 that he had kept in the trunk of the bureau's car, while Schmidt held a shotgun. Schmidt edged his way to the car's front door and slid in. He called his office, but no one answered. He called the Moosehead police. No answer.

4.

The Remos were not about to "come rampaging out," but continued to shake, scream, and shout.

"Ah! Ah! Ah! Ah!" screeched Letta Hudson in short barking jabs as she convulsed and fell to the floor.

Greta Clingmeier knelt by her side and the rest went silent.

Mr. and Mrs. Travers were terrified.

"We're ready for Jesus and them pearly gates!" Angle murmured.

"Amen!" intoned the Hudsons.

"How can you be thinking about pearly gates when those murderers are outside!?" Mrs. Travers found herself shouting.

Silence fell on the room.

"We're all going to be murdered!" she said.

"That's why we're ready fer t' see God face to face," said the reverend.

"You're just going to sit here while they're getting ready to shoot everybody here?"

"The Lord led us here to be swept up in clouds of glory."

"And how do you know this is the day?" insisted Mrs. Travers.

"Because the Lord said the end would come on July thirty-first."

"Well, he got the date wrong, because this is August first."

"It's the thirty-first."

"No. It's the first."

"The Lord does not make mistakes."

"Well, you did. Do you know what day of the week this is?"

"Saturday."

"Right, Saturday. Look at your cell phones for the date."

"We don't have none," said Jeb Hudson. "How about you?"

"It's in my purse in the car."

Now that the lights were off Charles Dinkins walked into the kitchen and felt for the wall calendar the women had hung earlier that day. He brought it into the living room.

"Anyone got a match?" he asked.

Jeb Hudson pulled a match pack out of his pocket and lit one.

Angle was silent. Others edged closer to Charles Dinkins, wanting a look.

"She's right," Dinkins said, and others murmured.

"The date don't matter," said Jeb Hudson. "Fact is we got people out there want to kill us. If that don't get us eternal life, I don't know what will." To punctuate his point he snorted, "Hunh!"

"Yeah, that's right!" said Carl Clingmeier and others agreed.

Reverend Angle drew himself up tall and looked at Charles Dinkins. "Anyone who does not believe that the Lord has sent us here to be taken up, in whatever way on whatever day, is free to go." He looked around. "If these folks"—the Traverses— "want to go, they can. No one's holdin' anyone here."

"Charles," said Mrs. Travers, "let's go." She stood and walked toward the back door.

"We can't walk out there," said Mr. Travers. "Those gunmen are waiting for us."

"Well, the childrens has got to go," said Mrs. Dinkins.

"There you go again with that!" shouted Carl Clingmeier.

"Well, I'm going!" Mrs. Travers said loudly, and ran out the back door.

Her husband stared briefly after her, then bolted out the door.

"Them strangers took off!" shouted Jeb Hudson.

Charles Dinkins said, "I'm takin' my childrens outta here too!" Mrs. Dinkins grabbed their children's hands and the family hurried out the door.

"They're leavin', reverend!" shouted Carl Clingmeier.

"Let 'em," said Reverend Angle. "They ain't fit fer salvation."

"What's that about the date?" asked Letta Hudson.

"Date don't mean nothin'," replied Reverend Angle. "Anti-Christ is outside in full force, that's what matters. That's yer sign."

"Maybe the date does mean sumthin'," said Jeb Hudson.

"Gotta mean a lot," said his wife.

"How d'you explain the forces of Anti-Christ if the date means everything?" asked the reverend. "God's message is comin' to me from five thousand billion miles away. Course it's gonna get tangled up in the comin'."

"He's got a point," Jeb said to his wife.

"If God was standin' right here in this room deliverin' His message," Angle asserted, "then it'd be diffrunt. But he ain't. He wasn't. He's speakin' all the way from Heaven. Course the message is gonna get tweeked a bit."

The Clingmeier girls were still crying.

"Mommy," said the eldest, "let's go."

"I don't want to be blown up!" said the younger.

Then both resumed crying.

"Would you shut them up!" snapped the reverend. "We're here witnessin' for the Lord! We don't need hysterics! This is a time for joy! A time for celebration! AMEN Praise JESus!!! Glory hallelujah!!!!!!"

"I'm so wrapped up in ecstasy, reverend," said Carl Clingmeier, "that I'm just bustin' with the Holy Spirit!"

Meanwhile Letta Hudson went over to the two Clingmeier children, put her arms around them, and whispered, "You two shouldn't be here. You come with me."

"Where?" asked the elder girl.

"We'll follow the Dinkinses."

"We cain't leave Ma," she sobbed.

Mrs. Hudson went over to Mrs. Clingmeier (who was standing in the middle of the room, hands raised, palms up, a beatific smile on her face) and said, "Greta." Mrs. Clingmeier paid her no heed. Mrs. Hudson repeated, "Greta." When Mrs. Clingmeier still did not respond, Mrs. Hudson shook her. "Listen to me," she said.

Mrs. Clingmeier looked at her.

"Greta! Your children! They've got to go!"

Mrs. Clingmeier smiled and said, "I know. Jesus is waiting."

"Yes, He's outside. And your children want to meet Him."

"Let us go to meet the Lord Jesus," said Mrs. Clingmeier, and began walking towards the open door. Mrs. Hudson scooted the children after their mother and followed them outside.

"Where is He?" Mrs. Clingmeier asked.

"Straight ahead," Mrs. Hudson replied.

The four kept walking.

5.

Outside the Remos' house, neither deputy Schmidt nor FBI agent Siggy Harris nor any of the journalists were aware that more than half of the building's occupants had left by the back door. In fact, because Harris was certain that the Remos were singing their death chant and about to "bust out," the deputy was nervous. He sat behind the wheel of his car, his heart palpitating and his hands trembling.

"Mister FBI," he called, leaning his head out the window to Harris, who was crouching at the back of the car.

"What?!"

"C'm here, would ya?"

"What!"

"Just c'm here."

"Did you make the call?"

It was too dark for Harris to see into the car.

"Yeah, I got the police on the phone. They want t'talk t'ya."

As Harris crawled towards the driver's door, Schmidt put the car in reverse. And as Harris pulled himself into a crouch and lifted an arm to receive the phone, Schmidt put his foot on the accelerator. The wheels spun gravel, the car hesitated for a moment, then raced backwards. Harris fell on his back.

Schmidt could see nothing. The county road was thirty feet behind him and he did not see the cluster of reporters blocking the end of the drive, gathered in a knot and talking.

The reporters heard the roar of an engine and saw tail-lights racing backwards and ran, but Schmidt, unable to see the driveway, swerved off the gravel and onto the highway. At that moment he heard a sickening thud and knew he had hit a reporter. He yanked the gear shift into "drive," swung the car around and tore off, not caring if he hit five reporters, just so long as he got the hell out of there.

At that moment Siggy Harris came running up the drive and down the road after the fast disappearing car. No one seemed to notice. Producers and journalists were milling about and shouting for their cameramen to get footage of their writhing colleague. One alert cameraman switched on a spotlight and the others grabbed their equipment and gathered in a tight knot around the injured reporter, who was screaming for an ambulance.

Keeping his wits about him, Gus Harvey's producer kept his production crew off to the side, as Harvey prepared to talk to the camera.

"At precisely ten-forty-five this evening, a sheriff's car with an unidentified driver came roaring backwards out of the driveway, veered and hit a BBC reporter, Phil Lewis. At this point, as you can see, pandemonium reigns."

Harvey's cameraman panned to the news crews bunched around Lewis and shouting questions. The camera panned back to Harvey, who was saying, "No one knows who was behind the wheel of that car. Was it the deputy sheriff or, more likely, one of the Remos making an escape? Where are the FBI agent and the deputy sheriff? Are the Remos now poised for a breakout? Or did the Remos overpower the lawmen and pack themselves inside the car and take off? The tension here is unbelievable."

6.

By the time Rex and Judy arrived at Dickie Wellstone's, the party was in full swing.

"Well, hel-l-l-o," Dickie bawled to them at the door. "It's the handsome twosome," he said and stepped aside to let them in. "Don't you look delicious as usual," he said, smiling at Judy. Turning to Rex he said, "Sally Lou's already here. So's hubby." As he steered them through the foyer into the living room he asked, "Drinks?"

"Yes," groused Rex, irritated to hear that Sally Lou had arrived first, possibly ruining their opportunity to exonerate themselves.

"What's your pleasure?" asked Dickie.

"Vodka tonic," said Judy.

"Same," Rex said.

While Dickie poured drinks, Rex scanned the room. Nearby several couples sat on chairs and couches. Further off he noticed Sally Lou's husband, Dirk, drink in hand and chest puffed out, talking to a shapely blonde. In the far corner he recognized Sally Lou surrounded by a knot of men and women. She was talking volubly.

Rex wished that he could reach out and place a band of invisible tape over her mouth. He started towards her. Then he noticed a short, stocky woman sticking her nose into Sally Lou's face and berating her while others laughed and snickered.

"What do you mean, Montana isn't a state?" he heard the accuser say. "I was born in Wyoming, you witless stick!"

As he noticed Sally Lou's eyes brimming with tears, Rex recognized the face of the accuser. Lou Amstatter!

As Rex moved towards the cluster of people surrounding Sally Lou, Amstatter was almost shouting, "You're everything that feminists have fought against for years."

"All right, what is going on here?" Rex asked, coming up to Sally Lou and putting an arm around her shoulders.

"You," Lou said to Rex, "are a toilet lid. The two of you together couldn't beat a rat on an I.Q. test."

"Well, thank you," Rex said, smiling broadly.

"So Montana's not a state, is it?"

"Of course it's a state. You didn't think we were serious this morning?"

"Sally Lou just said she wasn't sure if it was or not."

The snickering grew louder.

Rex led the sobbing Sally Lou towards Dirk, who was leaning into the blonde and talking earnestly.

"Hey, champ!" Rex called. "Yoh!"

Dirk's attention didn't waver.

"Hey, Dirk, boy!" Rex said.

Sally Lou broke away from Rex and rushed to Dirk, throwing her arms about him. The snickering in the corner burst into laughter. The startled blonde staggered back two paces, turned and walked off.

"What's the matter?" Dirk asked Sally Lou.

"Those horrible people wouldn't let me alone! They kept pestering me about Montana."

"What people?"

"Those!" Sally Lou said, pointing at the cluster.

"They were giving Sally Lou a hard time about the Montana business," Rex said.

"What Montana business?" Dirk asked.

"It's a long story," Rex replied. "They gave Sally Lou a kidding."

"That woman was mean and nasty!" Sally Lou said, pointing to Lou Amstatter, who now stood with the cluster of smirking guests.

Dirk tried masking his feeling of indifference by pulling her to him and saying, "Don't listen to them. Just walk away. They're jealous of you."

"That woman is HORrible! Ugh!!!!

"Well there, you see, she's jealous. She knows she's ugly and you're beautiful. Men adore you and hate her."

"That's Amstatter," Rex mumbled out the side of his mouth.

"Oh, Amstatter," Dirk acknowledged. "She's vicious, baby. Just vicious. Of course she's jealous: you've got talent. You sing like Joan Sutherland, act like Meryl Streep, and dance like Martha Graham."

During this recitation Sally Lou stopped sobbing, looked up at Dirk and smiled. "You think so?"

"I know so, baby. You're the greatest."

Sally Lou puckered up her lips, stood on her tippy toes and gave her husband a kiss.

"I'll find, Judy," Rex said, moving off.

"What's this Montana business, baby?" Dirk asked.

"Oh, we had this woman from Grand Tally on the show this morning with this map of the U.S. that didn't have Montana on it. Why? Why wouldn't it have Montana on it?"

"Didn't have Montana on it?"

"No. And she convinced us that Montana wasn't a state only I wasn't sure it wasn't a state but Rex and Jelton told me that it wasn't and said they didn't give a damn if it was or wasn't and ever since then people have been calling the network and calling us names. Rex told that awful woman that it was a gag, but she didn't believe him. God!!! This is the end of my career!!!!!"

Sally Lou began sobbing again.

"Hey, honey, it's not the end of the world. No one's gonna listen to that Amstatter hag, believe me. Everyone hates her. Even her mirror can't stand her."

Just then Rex returned with Judy and the two couples went out the door.

7.

Carl Clingmeier had been dancing around the room in short hops and skips, clapping his hands and shouting, "Gobble-ran-de-famzeiter-festinger," over and over, louder and louder. Beads of sweat popped from his brow. Suddenly he stopped, closed his eyes and bent over, nearly exhausted. Slowly, he wobbled his way across the room and leaned against a wall and looked around. In the moonlight, the room seemed half empty. His wife and girls were gone. The Dinkinses and their children were gone. The couple he'd picked up on the road were gone. But the Chews, the Hudsons, the Reverend Angle and George Slow Bear were still there, still praying out loud and shouting in tongues. No, wait, Mrs. Hudson was gone too.

He was seized with a sudden fright. What had happened to the others? Had they been stolen? Then he realized that the Lord had come for them! They'd been raised up, swept into heaven! The Rapture had come and he had not been chosen! He was not fit for salvation! He uttered a cry so agonizing and horrible that even the others, who were shouting and stamping their feet in abandon, were startled into silence. The others rushed to him.

Mr. Ping Ling Chew was on his knees beside Carl and calling, "Calr! Calr! What the matter? You sick?"

Carl's only answer was to begin gasping for breath.

"He sick," Ping Ling said, looking up at the others. "He velly sick. Maybe God punish him."

Carl stopped gasping long enough to say, "They're gone."

"Who gone?" Ping Ling asked.

"His wife, his daughters," said Reverend Angle. "And the Dinkinses."

The others looked around and for the first time the others' absence registered.

"They was swept up into Glory!" Carl said hoarsely between sobs. "The Rapture's come an' went. They went. They was selected, we wasn't. We wasn't fit fer Rapturin'."

"They wasn't carried up into heaven," Angle said in disgust. "They walked outa here. They turned their backs on God. They're the ones ain't fit for salvation!"

"No, no," Carl argued. "They was swept up in clouds of glory."

"No, they wasn't!" Angle shouted. "I told 'em t'stay. They wouldn't listen. They walked outa here! I seen 'em!"

Carl sat up. "Walked outa here?"

"Walked? More like ran! Right out that door," Angle said, pointing.

"Why didn't they wait fer me?" Carl asked himself. "Why didn't they tell me they was goin'?" He never doubted for a moment that Greta and the children loved him. Something bad must have happened, something bad involving the Dinkinses and the other couple. He began to panic.

"You wanna know why they didn't tell you where they was goin'? Cause God has you marked for heaven and them for hell," the reverend said. "They're marchin' straight off t'hell."

"No, they ain't. They're in trouble and they need me." Carl scrambled to his feet and rushed out the open back door.

"Behold a blackened soul rushing off to its infernal reward!" warned Reverend Angle, pointing a long, skinny finger at the fleeing Clingmeier. "The soul is drawn like a magnet to its true home! Some runs straight to hell fire, burning pitch, and howling devils, others fly to the shining lights and golden streets of heaven! The Lord is makin' the great cut right now!"

"Say," said Mr. Hudson, looking around, "where is Letta?"

"Must have walked out too," said Slow Bear, realizing for the first time that Mrs. Hudson was gone.

"Plaise Jesus," said Mrs. Chew. "His saints is going home."

"Amen," said her husband.

"Amen!!!" added Reverend Angle, and he and the Chews spontaneously began singing:

"I'm headed up to heaven
An' will see those pearly gates,
Oh I'm goin' up to heaven
To see Jesus at the gates."

While they sang, Jeb Hudson, thunderstruck, wandered over to the door, shocked to learn that his wife would also leave without a word. Suddenly her head appeared inside the door. He jumped in surprise, as his wife put a finger to her mouth and waved for him to join her. Without looking back, Mr. Hudson stepped outside.

CHAPTER NINE

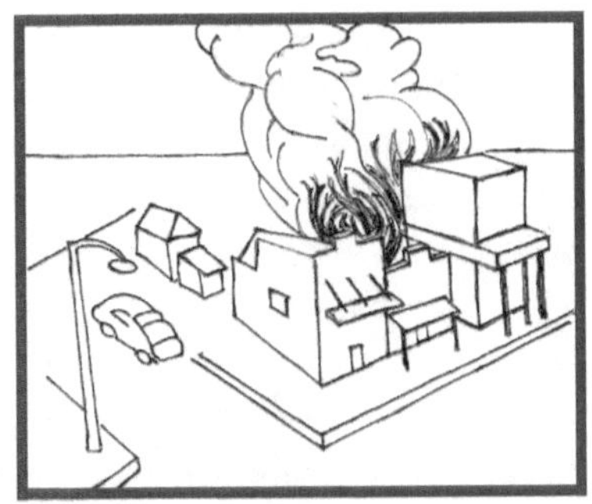

By one a.m. Eastern Daylight Time, when most East Coast residents were safely tucked in bed, Monica Clapper and Thornton Granger were coming to an end of their labors, printing the last copies of their press release. Tomorrow morning they would send it by express messenger to the major New York media outlets. From their office, high atop a midtown Manhattan skyscraper, hundreds of offices, north and south, were lit in spectacular array.

Ten blocks north, Rex and Judy, Dirk and Sally Lou were grabbing their coats and leaving Dickie Wellstone's.

A half hour's drive away on Long Island, Lorene and Jeannie, tired and bedraggled, stepped off the plane at LaGuardia Airport.

At the same time, Siggy Harris was on the phone with Jay Ritchie, asking when FBI reinforcements would arrive. Out in the countryside, Sheriff Brandt and Deputy Holman, having cut their bonds, were hobbling along the darkened dirt road towards Highway 25, where they hoped to snag a ride to Moosehead. Deputy Schmidt, who had backed out of the Remo's drive, was driving furiously down Highway 25 without any idea of where he was headed.

The Remos, for the most part, were scattered over the landscape, moving as quickly as they could in the dark to escape their assailants. Only the Reverend Angle and Mr. and Mrs. Chew remained in the house.

Simultaneously, the Montana Militia was driving slowly and noisily in its three broken vehicles towards Buck's home. Only by the merest of chances did they avoid encountering the twenty-three cars and pickups driven helter skelter across Rosebud County by the patrons of Sidewinders Bar & Grille.

And lastly, on a backstreet of Moosehead, secret agents agents Ez Lawson and Alan Bird were siphoning gas from a pickup into several coffee cans.

2.

Lorene and Jeannie took a bus to Port Authority Terminal in Manhattan. At two a.m. the station was deserted. The food shops were closed with their metal gates pulled down. Ticket windows were shut. The women felt alone and lost, exhausted and dispirited.

"Where we gonna get a place?" Lorene wondered, dragging her heavy bag behind her as she made her way towards a set of doors.

"Any place," said Jeannie, barely able to follow her. "Just ask anyone to name a hotel."

"Ask who?"

"Anyone."

They stood on the sidewalk outside, looking at the tall lighted buildings with billboards the likes of which they had only seen in magazines or movies. A few cars sped down the wide avenue in front of them.

"Gawd this is big," Lorene gasped.

"We gotta be careful, Lorene. You can't trust no one here."

"You think?"

"Yeah. We better find a cop."

"I can't walk that far. I can't walk anywhere."

"Wanna sit for a bit?"

"Yeah."

They sat on the sidewalk near the terminal entrance. Lorene closed her eyes and tried to sleep.

"Lorene," Jeannie said, "don't go to sleep. You gotta keep awake." As she said this, Jeannie yawned.

The two women sat next to each other, shoulder to shoulder, heads bowed and eyes closed, snoring softly.

3.

Hank Lambert, Governor of the state of Montana slept fitfully beside his wife. At twelve-o-five a.m. the Lamberts' bedside phone rang. On the fifth ring, the governor's eyes opened and he reached slowly for the receiver.

"Yes?"

"Sorry to wake you, governor."

"Mark?"

"Yes, sir," answered Mark Hotwell, Lambert's special assistant. "We have an emergency."

"What is it?" the governor asked, sitting up.

"The Remos, sir."

"What of them?"

"Well, they just kidnapped a Rosebud County deputy sheriff, took off in his car, and critically injured a news reporter."

"Where are they headed?"

"We don't know. It appears that most are still holed up in their bunker."

"Bunker? That's a house."

"Looks like a house, sir, but it was fortified by some members before the rest moved in. Right now there's only one FBI agent holding them off. His partner was evacuated hours ago. Sir, it gets worse. The Remos have set fire to several buildings and a car in Moosehead. The Moosehead fire department is fighting the blaze right now."

"How do you know they did it?"

"Your attorney general got an anonymous tip on his cell phone!"

"What!?"

"That was fifteen minutes ago. Ten minutes ago the fires started in Moosehead."

"What do you think we should do?"

"Call out the National Guard, Governor."

Lambert thought about it.

"Sir," Mark said, "we don't want the death of one more FBI

agent on our hands and we don't want a town butchered."

"Of course not. But what's the FBI doing about it?"

"I don't know, sir. They may not have the firepower to stop this group."

"All right, Mark. Call up the guard. Have them mobilize immediately with whatever it will take to stop this bunch."

"Right, sir."

Lambert hung up the phone and turned to his wife, who was listening.

"Why are you calling up the National Guard?"

"It's that cult. They're trying to burn down Moosehead."

"Oh, my God."

Lambert put on his dressing gown and slippers and went downstairs to make coffee.

4.

The call to the state's attorney general had, in fact, been made by Ez Lawson. Bird and Lawson's agency was a bitter rival to the FBI. The rivalry started after an FBI agent stumbled on the existence of this highly secretive agency, and the bureau tried using political pressure to dismantle it.

Lawson heard that Kline had been evacuated. No doubt Harris had already called for FBI backup, which would arrive before long. In order to embarrass the FBI, Lawson had gotten the Montana attorney general's cell phone number and told him that the Remos intended to burn down Moosehead. To make sure the attorney general believed it, Bird and Lawson had set fire to several abandoned buildings on the outskirts of town. The fire went quickly out of control, spread across dried grass and attacked a retail store. Just as a parked car exploded, Lawson and Bird were speeding out of Moosehead.

5.

Reverend Angle sat in an arm chair, pondering. He had said nothing for twenty minutes since the last defectors had left. He was beginning to doubt the Lord's revelations.

"Cheel up!" said Ping Ling Chew to his leader. "Don't ret those peopre bothel you. They headed straight for herr!"

Reverend Angle looked up briefly but said nothing.

"God told you today was Day of Judgment! Today we go heaven!" Chew said.

"Yes!" Chew's wife chorused. "Today we see puh-ley gates."

"Puh-ley gates!" Chew repeated.

"I got the date wrong," the reverend said glumly.

"No, it like you say. Message come long way from heaven. Get mixed in tlansit. You light. You light." Chew nodded vigorously and smiled broadly.

Suddenly, as Reverend Angle looked at the man and woman smiling and nodding, getting killed with two dimwitted illegals didn't seem so appealing. He put his head in his hands. Was he wrong about this business? He tried thinking it through again. He thought to himself, "Was it God I heard and saw?" He remembered the sudden light and the figure that approached him outside his house and warned him of the Day of Judgment and told him to travel west. Could that have been one of the dark angels? Could it have been the Evil One himself? He shuddered, thinking of what he had, perhaps, encountered. If it had been the Evil One, everything he had said and done since that encounter had been a terrible mistake. He was uncertain of everything except that he was about to die. And for what? For a mistake. He stood, looked at the open back door and made for it.

"Levelend Angre! Levelend Angre!" cried the Chews, hastening after their leader. "Where you going? Wait fol us!"

6.

At two a.m. Mountain States Time, the first FBI agents arrived from Coeur d'Aline, Idaho. These were twelve men with bullet-proof vests and rifles that could shoot through armor plating. They immediately pushed back the press, which had been slowly inching closer to the house. When he saw their rifles and grim faces, not even Gus Harvey tried bluffing them, but moved obediently back to the road with the other journalists.

Thirty-five minutes later another cadre of agents arrived, and for the next two hours they continued pouring in. Some arrived in trucks with lights and generators and set up a glare of spotlights covering the house.

The agent in charge, J.T. Baker, asked Harris, "Where the hell are the local officers?"

"The sheriff hasn't responded to calls. One deputy came, but he fled."

J.T. grunted in disgust, as if to say, "What else would you expect?" and turned away. Baker, like the other newly arrived agents, had a dark blue nylon jacket with "FBI" written in large yellow letters on the back. Even though it was night, he wore sun glasses.

"How many agents are here?" he bellowed to no one in particular.

"Sixty-three before you and your men arrived," answered a young agent.

"Where the hell are they?"

"They've surrounded the building, sir."

"Well, hooray for something done right," J.T. said sarcastically. "What's your name, junior?"

"Amos Brackston, sir."

"Well, Mr. Brackston, you are going to see some nasty shooting, unless I miss my guess. Ever seen a bloodbath before?"

"No, sir."

"Well, haul up your skirts and get ready, 'cause the blood is going to flow. Believe me."

"Uh, maybe they'll surrender."

"Brackston, you are so green they couldn't burn you for firewood. How long you been with the agency?"

"This is my first month."

"Damn! That long?"

"Yes, sir."

"How the hell did you get through the academy?"

"Hard work, sir."

"Was that it? Hard work? You don't have an uncle or cousin who's a U.S. senator?"

"No."

"You better move back away from the line of fire. Get back towards those reporters. But don't talk to 'em! Not a word. Understand?"

"Yes."

As Amos Brackston moved away, J.T. called out: "Henry Johnson! Is Henry Johnson here?"

Another agent said, "I believe he's in back of the house, sir."

"Go tell him I want him."

Minutes later Henry Johnson, a fifty-something, tired looking man with a drooping mustache trudged up to J.T.

"Henry Johnson, my name is J.T. Baker."

"I heard you were coming."

"You see any action from the back of the house?"

"Nothing."

"I have a profile of every person in that house, except the abductees. A black couple, two white couples, a Korean couple, one Indian, and three children."

"Plus the abductees."

"Plus the abductees."

"What's your plan?" Johnson asked

"I'm going to address them with a bull horn and try to persuade them to release the children and hostages."

"And if they don't?"

J.T. Baker said nothing.

Johnson shrugged. "It's your call. What do you want me to do?"

"Go back where you were. Wait. And keep your cell phone handy."

"Will do," Johnson said, turned and walked off.

7.

As Dirk and Sally Lou headed cross town in their cab on Forty-Second Street past Port Authority, Lorene and Jeannie sat slumped on the sidewalk near the corner. Several hookers and a pimp had convened there and were talking loudly as a patrol car pulled up to the curb. The two cops inside noted the two sleeping figures and stepped out; one of them prodded Lorene with his nightstick.

"Wake up."

"Huh?"

"Wake up."

The three hookers and the pimp ceased their chatter and focused on the pending drama.

Lorene did not move or open her eyes. The cop prodded harder. This time she opened her eyes and yelped.

"On your feet," the cop barked.

"Ooh-ooh," one of the hookers said.

The second cop jabbed Jeannie with his stick.

"Cut it out!" Jeannie snapped, coming awake and waving her arms.

The hookers laughed.

"On yer feet!" the first cop repeated.

"Go aWAY!" Lorene said.

"Get up!" the second cop ordered. "I said get up."

Lorene groaned and rolled onto her hands and knees.

"UP!" the second cop repeated.

"Oh, no," said another hooker and clucked her tongue, "I think they're in trouble."

Jeannie got to her knees and swayed.

"How long have you ladies been drinking?" asked the first cop.

"We're not drinking," Lorene said, as she struggled to stand, but failed.

"We're taking you two in," said the first cop.

Jeannie rolled back down on the sidewalk.

The pimp and hookers laughed.

The first cop grabbed Lorene and tried pulling her to her feet. "This one weighs a ton," he told his partner. "Give me a hand."

The two men lifted her. The first led her to the patrol car, while the other pried Jeannie off the ground, twisted her arm behind her back and pushed her into the car as the pimps and hookers laughed and called and called, "Watch yerself, baby!"

CHAPTER TEN

As Lorene and Jeannie were being hauled to the drunk tank, Cap and the boys were still slowly making their way across country.

"Cap," said Buck, "we ain't in no shape to whup a sick dawg."

Buck was right, Cap thought.

"We got our tails 'tween our legs, and we best git home to lick our wounds. Bouncer's ole lady and my Lorene, either one, could settle our hash right now."

"Yer right," Cap agreed. "We'll rest up tonight an' tomorra figur' what t'do."

2.

Meanwhile, the 143 volunteers from Moosehead's six bars were still driving in every direction across Rosebud County in search of the gunmen who had torn up Sheriff's Brandt's office and made off with Lew Mitchell. None of the searchers were more eager to have the first shot at the jail breakers than Brenda Snavely and her live-in boyfriend Bobby Banks.

"Put yer foot to th' pedal, Bobby," Brenda shouted.

"Ah'm doin' sixty-five," Bobby retorted. "Can't drive faster'n that on gravel. We'll end up with our feet 'n the air."

Neither Bobby nor Brenda had the slightest idea who had committed the crime or where to look for them. Like the other vigilantes, they were driving helter skelter across the county.

"Whoever done it gotta be from here," Brenda said.

"Open that glove compartment, would ya," said Bobby.

"You hear what I said?"

"Yeah, I heard it."

"Well?"

"Makes sense t' me. Open the glove compartment."

Brenda complied and handed Bobby a pint of bourbon. Bobby unscrewed the cap, took a snort and handed it to Brenda.

"I know they're from this county," Brenda said. "They have to be. They knew Lew Mitchell, and from what the dispatcher said, they was all friends." She took a swig.

"That's right!" Bobby said, as the truth of it dawned on him.

"Wait a second!" Brenda snapped. "I know who it was! Those Remos, Remies, whatever they're called. That bunch that was on TV that shot the FBI guy."

"They're not from here, sweet cheeks," Bobby countered. "So how'd they know Lew Mitchell?"

"They came here 'cause they must've had some kind of deal with Mitchell. Must've known him from before."

Brenda took the bottle from Bobby and took a pull. The pickup went over a hump in the road and bounced a foot in the air.

"Shit," said Brenda, "I wonder what the hell's going on at the Randall place."

"Huh?"

"That's where them Remies are fighting it out with the FBI."

"You figure that's where they'd go?"

"Course they would! Get us back to Highway 25."

Without a word, Bobby slammed his foot on the brake, spinning the pickup around180 degrees. He shoved it back into first gear and took off.

Driving on Highway 25, several miles from the Randall place, Bobby and Brenda saw searchlights scanning the sky. As they neared County Road X15 they encountered a roadblock and the flashing lights of police vehicles, with cars and vans parked on both sides of the highway and people standing around in clusters. There were cameras, police, microphones, flashing lights.

Three state troopers in the middle of the road signaled them to pull over.

Bobby rolled down his window. "What's up?"

"Park over there," a trooper said, pointing. "Don't get out."

"Shit this is big time," Brenda told Bobby as he pulled over.

The trooper walked up to Bobby's window.

"Is this on account of them religious nuts?" Bobby asked.

The trooper said, "I need to see your drivers' licenses."

Bobby and Brenda reached for their wallets.

As Brenda handed her license to the trooper she said, "Do you know about the raid on the sheriff's office in Moosehead?"

"What raid?"

"A bunch of guys came in there, sprung a prisoner, and smashed the radio. That's what we come to tell ya."

"We didn't get any calls on that."

"That's because the dispatch radio got busted up."

"Did you see this happen?"

"No, we heard it from the dispatcher. And no one can get hold of the sheriff or the deputies."

"When did this happen?"

"Hours ago."

"You two sit tight."

The trooper walked back into the road.

Bobby started counting the parked cars. "There's fifteen cars they've flagged down. Must be 'cause of the standoff."

"Beats me. What time is it?"

Bobby flipped on the overhead light and looked at his watch. "Two fourteen."

Just then they heard a droning and looked up to see floodlights coming at them. And then the noise of big engines.

"Shit, what the hell is that?" Brenda asked.

The lights got brighter and the engines louder and then they could see armored vehicles and trucks coming towards them. As the convoy turned onto County Road X15 Bobby and Brenda saw that the trucks were filled with soldiers in mufti.

"They're headed for the Randall place," Bobby said.

Just then they could hear engines and rotary blades overhead and saw searchlights, and suddenly a large track of the land and road ahead were illuminated as two helicopters followed the convoy.

"Shit," Brenda gasped, "this is bigger stuff than I thought."

The trooper was still in the middle of the road, talking with two other officers.

"They ain't doin' nothin' with that information," Bobby said. "I want t' tell someone but I can't. They'll see me get out of the car. But they won't see you if you sneak out and tell some of them reporters."

"What difference is that goin' t' make if them Remies has already snuck back here?"

"Supposin' they haven't. They might be somewhere else raisin' hell."

"You're right," Brenda said decisively and opened the door a crack. She gave a glance at the troopers and scooted out, walking quickly to the van ahead. At the front of the van, Gus Harvey, his producer, and a cameraman were talking.

"Excuse me," she said.

They stopped talking and looked at her.

"You all are reporters?"

"Yes," Harvey said.

"I want you to know that I just come from town where a bunch of these Remies went into the sheriff's office, smashed up the dispatch radio and freed a prisoner. They was armed and their faces was smeared with coal dust or somethin'."

"Did you see this?" the producer asked.

"I heard it from the dispatcher just after it happened."

"Would you mind being interviewed?" Harvey asked.

"Hell, no."

"Good," the producer said. "Would you please move over here, to the edge of the road, in the light."

Brenda complied and the cameraman raised his camera as she told Harvey the story. " . . . the dispatcher said their faces were blackened an' they came in with guns, smashed up the dispatch radio, and freed a prisoner."

"Do you have any reason to believe these were Remos?"

"They had t'be. Who else woulda done it? We didn't have no trouble here outside a few Saturday night bar fights. No sir, we didn't have no trouble in this town till the Remies come here."

"What was the dispatcher's reaction?"

"She was shittin' in her jeans."

"We can't say that on camera. How else would you describe her reaction?"

"Her eyes was big as saucers and she could barely speak."

"Did they threaten to kill her?"

"I can't say. But they was pointin' rifles at her."

Harvey lowered the microphone. "Thank you. That was excellent."

Brenda snuck back to the pickup.

Gus Harvey said to the cameraman, "Let's wrap it."

The cameraman focused on Harvey who said, "That story indicates that the Remo cult may be much larger than law enforcement guessed. And it appears that they are also heavily armed and extremely dangerous.

"In the event you just tuned in, the Montana National Guard has just arrived with helicopters and five armored vehicles, which now surround the Remos' bunker."

A minute later that raw footage was headed via satellite to New York.

3.

Sally Lou lay awake in bed for hours, tossing and turning as she replayed the events at Dickie Wellstone's. Strident voices kept shouting at her, while sneering faces leered. Amstatter—short, squat Amstatter—was laughing at her. Sally Lou pressed her hands against her eyes and temples, trying to squeeze Amstatter out of her mind. Amstatter kept yelling, "What do you mean, Montana isn't a state? I was born in Wyoming, you witless stick! . . . You've set the Women's Movement back fifty years! . . . You, couldn't beat a rat on an I.Q. test! . . . I.Q. TEST! I.Q. TEST!

I.Q. TEST! I.Q. TEST!"

Dirk was lying next to her, snoring peacefully. Sally Lou looked at Dirk and considered what he had said about Amstatter. Was he right? Was Amstatter jealous of her? May-be. Amstatter was really ugly. She was vicious too. Everyone knew that.

Amstatter had to be jealous of her. Sally Lou got hundreds of fan letters a week. Of course some people called her names, accusing her of insensitivity, of not caring about anyone but herself and her family, saying she talked too much about her daughter, writing the nastiest things because of that fat farm, calling her stupid! There was that word again! "Stupid."

She flopped onto her side and dug her fingers into the pillow. Her mistake about Montana, that desert or whatever it was, would be all over the tabloids! Shit! Now there would be more nasty letters and the show's ratings would drop.

Sally Lou tossed again, but Dirk continued snoring peacefully.

4.

As Brenda Snavely unfolded the Moosehead drama to Gus Harvey, the trooper to whom she had spoken saw a young man with an FBI jacket. The agent was Amos Brackston.

The trooper walked hurriedly to Brackston. "Sir," he said, "I've got some important information."

Brackston, who had never been called "sir" before, straightened himself. "What?" he asked.

"The sheriff's office in Moosehead was broken into about forty minutes ago. A dozen men with rifles smashed up the dispatch radio and freed a prisoner." The trooper added, "They may have been another bunch of Remos."

Brackston's eyes popped. "Jeez!" he said. He pulled out his walkie-talkie. "Mr. Baker?"

"Yeah!?" Baker barked.

"This is Brackston, sir. We just got word that the sheriff's office in Moosehead was attacked by a dozen men with rifles who took the prisoner."

"Who told you that?"

"State police, sir. They think those men may have been Remos."

"Where are the attackers now?"

"No one knows."

"Who told you this?"

"A state trooper."

"Is he there?"

"Yes, sir."

"Tell him to stay put. I'll be right there."

Two minutes later Baker and General Amos Butts of the Montana National Guard stood with Brackston and the state trooper, pumping him for information. The state trooper suddenly turned, looked at the crowd gathering on the opposite side of the road and pointed to Brenda Snavely.

5.

Alicia Clapper and Thornton Granger were reviewing their last twelve hours of work.

"Press release is done," said Granger.

"Check," said Clapper.

"And ready to go to the major outlets by messenger when business resumes."

"Check," Clapper reiterated.

"We emailed two dozen radio and television talk show hosts, offering an interview with Feinstein or Driggs."

"Check. And with their lawyer."

"With Tarlton Smithers, their lawyer."

At Clapper and Grangers' insistence, Smithers had visited Grand Tally offices that afternoon for a briefing to prepare him for interviews. Most interviews were a piece of cake, but the network morning news shows often didn't call until five a.m. and expected you to wake up, shower, shave, dress and get over to a studio in two hours. Smithers was more than willing to do it (interviews were advertising) and was better at it than most.

Granger poured himself another cup of coffee from the carafe and glanced at the clock. One-thirty a.m. For the last six hours he and Clapper had been writing down talking points for Feinstein, Driggs, and Smithers.

"One thing we didn't do," Clapper said.

"What's that?"

"Make those two TV dimwits apologize on air for insinuating that the U.S. map was a piece of shit."

"That squirrely guy just about said it was."

"Everyone knows what he meant."

Clapper and Granger had watched a copy of "The Rex and Sally Lou Show" and heard Rex tell Ms. Rates that "Your map is a piece of shhhh—" Rex had censored himself, but it was clear what he meant to say.

"You're right. We gotta get him—them— to make an on-air apology. If they don't, Grand Tally will sue. Big time."

"Who the hell are those two turkeys, anyway?"

"I don't know. Doesn't matter. Let's finish the check list. I want to get some sleep. Tomorrow's going to be another long day."

6.

At that moment J.T. Baker was questioning Brenda Snavely. "How do you know that the men who broke into the sheriff's office were Remos?"

Brenda didn't like Baker's tone. "I didn't say they were, did I?" She glared at him. "But it's pretty damn coincidental," she continued, "that the break-in happens while you've got your hands full with this bunch." She paused. "Isn't it?"

"Get her out of here!"

An FBI agent took Snavely's arm and led her to the side of the road.

Another agent, Sandra Moser, approached Baker. "Sir," she said, "state patrol just radioed information on a three-pickup-two-car pileup on this highway, about fifteen miles south. No bodies, no victims. The cars and pickups were empty. Think we should send an agent?"

"How about you? Got a vehicle?"

"No."

"Will you drive her?" Baker asked a state trooper.

Moments later Moser was riding in a state patrol car driven by trooper Clyde Hammer to the accident scene. In ten minutes they were facing a mass of twisted metal and shattered glass scattered across the road. While Moser searched the scene, Hammer used his car's computer to discover the vehicles' owners. Within minutes they had names and addresses.

7.

The scattered groups of Remos called to one another in the dark. The Reverend Angle heard voices far ahead of him, but he chose to move in another direction. He was intent on shaking off the Chews, who were calling, "Wait up! Wait up! You wark too fas'!"

The reverend turned and stopped. "Go away! . . . Go Away! . . . Follow the others! Follow them!" Angle pointed in one direction and ran in another.

Neither the Hudsons, the Clingmeiers, George Slow Bear, the Harrises and Dinkinses knew where they were headed, but were spurred by the fear that any moment a helicopter's searchlights would suddenly pin them in its beam.

CHAPTER ELEVEN

State trooper Clyde Hammer and FBI agent Sandra Moser were driving down Highway 25 to Buck Simpson's house when two vehicles appeared on the horizon, driving slowly towards them. As the lead vehicle approached, they saw that it veered side to side.

"That guy's got a load on," Hammer said switched on his car's flashing lights.

Alfred immediately stepped on the brake and pulled over. Cap swung behind him as the police car made a U turn. Cap stepped out of his truck. Fortunately for Cap and his men, they had washed the charcoal dust from their faces after springing Lew Mitchell.

"Get back in," Hammer said, approaching Cap's pickup.

Cap ignored him, pretending to be frightened, talking loudly and nervously. "You gotta help us. I gotta get my friends to a hospital." He gestured to the back of the pickup.

Hammer peered over the side. Three bandaged men lay there.

"What happened to them?" Moser asked, looking at the bleeding men.

"We was waylaid," Cap answered. "Some guys came at us an' smashed our cars an' pickups."

"What d'ya mean?" Hammer asked.

"We was drivin' t'm' friends house when two pickups come racin' up behind us, rode our tails fer about a mile, then swung around us and run into our two lead vee-hicles. We had us one hell of a five vee-hicle pileup with cars an' pickups and m'friends thrown out. You can see what happened." He closed in a rush, pointing at the men lying on the pickup bed, then added, "Lookit what those crazies done to our vee-hicles."

"Was that your pileup eight miles down the road?" Moser asked.

"Yeah, that was us," Buck interjected, sticking his head out the cab window.

"Who're you?" Hammer asked.

"Buck Simpson."

"So you're Simpson," Hammer said. "Explain to me why you're drivin' towards the accident."

"We went to my house to hide," Buck explained. "Then decided we better get medical help."

"I'm calling an ambulance," Hammer said and walked to the state car.

Moser, meanwhile, asked, "Can you describe the vehicles that ran you off the road?"

"I remember they was out-of-state plates," Cap said. "I got a look at the men in one of the vee-hicles and their faces was all black, like smeared with soot."

"Sounds like the group that broke into the sheriff's office," Moser said. To herself she added out loud, "Must be more Remos than anyone thought."

"That's for sure," Cap said.

2.

At five a.m. the 43rd precinct station in midtown Manhattan was beginning to stir. A new shift was coming on duty and voices in the halls and offices began filtering into the holding cell. No one in the cell was making noise, except for Lorene, who lay on her stomach, snoring. Of the four women in lockup, only one was awake, a redhead who sat on the edge of her bunk, smoking.

Another woman turned and shifted as she drifted in and out of sleep. Lorene's snoring grew louder. The woman shifted again and pulled the blanket over her head. Lorene sputtered and went silent. The redhead who was smoking aimed her cigarette at the lidless toilet that sat between her bunk and Lorene's, and sent the cigarette arcing into the air. It landed on the porcelain rim smeared with dried feces and slid into the water. She pulled at a strand of her hair as she looked at the other figures.

With a sudden explosive burst, Lorene resumed snoring and Jeannie joined in. The woman drifting in and out of sleep came awake.

"Knock it off!" she barked at them.

The snoring continued.

"I said knock it off!" she repeated, only louder.

Lorene kept sleeping. Jeannie sat bolt upright. "What!?" she demanded.

Lorene gave a few snorts.

The woman who had shouted, "Knock it off," flicked off her blanket, pulled back a leg, then shot it out, hitting Lorene in the butt.

"Ahhh!!" Lorene yelped, coming awake. She saw the woman glaring at her.

"I was talkin' to you," said the woman.

Lorene saw her angry look. "What?" she asked.

"Knock off the snoring, I want to sleep."

Lorene nodded. Jeannie said nothing, trying to size up the situation, but it was hard. Her head was pounding.

After the woman lay down, Lorene slowly relaxed. She didn't dare go to sleep for fear of snoring again. She was thirsty; her mouth was dry, her head hurt. She looked around the cell but did not see a sink. She did not dare speak to Jeannie, and Jeannie did not dare speak to her. They both lay down, waiting for someone to unlock the cell door, whenever that might be.

3.

By six a.m. Mountain Standard Time several hundred onlookers were gathered by barriers that state police had erected on county road X15, a quarter mile either side from the Randall place. Two helicopters circled ominously overhead with continuous chopping sounds, while below a dozen armored vehicles and hundreds of National Guard troops and FBI agents surrounded the house. The onlookers waited.

What they could not know was that J.T. Baker was arguing fiercely with Colonel Amos Sledge of the Montana National Guard over who was in charge at the standoff.

Sledge was red-faced and stabbing his finger in Baker's chest and yelling, "I'll tell you, mister, that you do not run this state. You do not come into Montana and start tellin' us what to do. Not now, not never!"

Baker was glaring and began shouting, "You goddamn better follow procedure. You do not command this situation."

"Tell me," Sledge shouted back, "what you or your men have accomplished in ten hours, besides getting a toe shot off. That's it! That's all you did! I'd laugh if this situation wasn't a powder keg."

"Mister. . ." Baker began, drawing out the word in a threatening manner.

Before he could finish, Sledge turned and waved him off.

"Don't you turn your back on me, mister!" Baker shouted.

"Kiss my ass," Sledge replied quietly, still walking.

Baker pulled out his cell phone and called Spencer Hardwicke at FBI headquarters and Sledge opened his cell phone and called Governor Lambert.

A few minutes later, Gus Harvey was taping a report for New York.

". . . You can see the crowds gathering here about a quarter mile from the standoff. The pickups and cars started coming before dawn and they're still arriving. About three hundred people are now waiting anxiously to view the fate of the Remos, who are still hunkered down inside their bunker.

"There has not been one word or sign from the Remos in twelve hours. But the FBI has now confirmed that another group of Remos has been terrorizing Moosehead and the surrounding countryside. First came an attack on the Rosebud County sheriff's office early last evening. A dozen men with rifles freed several prisoners and destroyed the entire office. Hours later, two stores and several buildings in downtown Moosehead were destroyed by fire. Arson is suspected.

"Then, early this morning five vehicles were ambushed on a state highway, causing a major pileup and severely injuring a dozen persons.

"In the meantime, everyone is expecting the FBI or National Guard momentarily to issue an ultimatum to the Remos, but there has been no word from the Christian cultists now surrounded in their garrison."

4.

As Harvey finished, J.T. Baker climbed into an armored vehicle and drove within fifty feet of the house. The armored vehicle had a speaker attached to its roof. Safely seated inside, Baker lifted a microphone to his mouth.

"Attention Remos! . . . You are completely surrounded. There is no escape. If you attempt any violence, we will respond."

5.

Charlie and Olivia Travers were walking as quickly as they dared in the early dawn. Occasionally they heard voices somewhere behind them. Mrs. Travers, gasping for breathe, suddenly stopped, pushed out her chest and inhaled as deeply as possible. She rummaged in her bag for her inhaler.

"Take your time, Olivia, we're far enough away now," Charles said. "Whoever was shooting at the house won't follow us."

She did not answer but shook the inhaler, put one end in her mouth, squeezed and held the mist in her lungs. She repeated it once more. Shaking, she finally said, "All right. Let's go."

6.

At that moment, Sheriff Brandt and Deputy Holman were hobbling alongside Highway 25.

"I don't like walkin' so close to the road, sheriff," Holman complained. "Them sonsofbitches might come back any minute."

"We'll see 'em. All we gotta do is dive into some brush."

"But there ain't no brush."

Holman's whiney voice was getting on Brandt's nerves.

"Just shut up."

"Okay."

Although he talked boldly, Brandt was just as apprehensive as Holman. What his deputy said was true. This stretch of road offered no hiding place, no more than low lying clumps of grass on slightly rolling land, a poor concealment should anyone drive slowly by, searching for them. But Brandt felt they had no choice. They needed to get to a phone and alert state police. Who were those men who had ambushed them?

"We'll wait here," Brandt said. "Sooner or later someone's bound to come by."

"You want t' take a chance on meetin' up with those fellas again?" Holman asked. "We ain't got our pistols, we ain't got a rifle, we ain't got a shotgun. We got piss."

"Aren't many people travelin' this time of morning."

Just then a pair of headlights appeared in the distance, coming from Moosehead. Both men watched as the light approached.

"It's only one car," Brandt said.

"Could be some of the gang, sheriff."

"Yer right," Brandt agreed.

"Why don't we play it safe and get off the road?"

Both men hobbled off the road, looking for a tall clump of grass when the car stopped.

A voice called, "That you, Brandt?"

Brandt turned and asked, "Who're you?"

"Need help?"

"Who're you?"

"Jim McFarland."

The name meant nothing to Brandt, but the tone of the man's voice reassured him. He started back towards the road.

Holman stayed put.

McFarland noticed the sheriff's torn and dirt covered clothes and asked, "What the hell happened?"

"We got ambushed." Brandt turned his head and called to Holman, "Get up here!"

Holman began walking towards the car.

Brandt got in the passenger side.

"Ambushed?" McFarland asked.

"About twenty of 'em. Heavily armed."

"You musta got hit by the gang that's holed up at the Randall place and busted out two of yer prisoners."

"Busted out our prisoners? What're you talkin' about?"

"A gang of Remos come into yer office an' busted out two prisoners."

"We had one guy in lockup," Brandt said.

"Don't you know what the hell happened to your office?"

"What're you talkin' about?"

"A bunch of Remos come in, freed two prisoners and busted up yer dispatch radio and beat up the operator."

"SHIT!"

Holman was alongside the car.

"Get in!!" Brandt ordered.

"The state police is already out after this gang," McFarland said. "The FBI and National Guarde got 'em surrounded at the Randall place."

"Head for there," Brandt said.

McFarland sped off, saying, "You two musta got ambushed by the same group. They shot an FBI agent. Killed him and began shootin' at the reporters out there. Even run one of 'em over with a car."

"Who're you talkin' about?" Holman wanted to know.

"The guys that got you two. They're surrounded at the Randall place."

"You think they're the ones that hog-tied us?" Holman asked.

"Must've been," Brandt mused to himself.

"Hog-tied you?" McFarland asked in astonishment.

"Yeah!" Holman began, but Brandt cut him off, with, "Ambushed us."

"Your deputy said 'hog-tied'."

"Ambushed."

7.

The gang that had hogtied Sheriff Brandt and Deputy Holman was in sad shape. All but Cap and Bouncer now lay in beds in Moosehead's Veterans Memorial Hospital with intravenous feeding and morphine tubes plugged into their arms. A few were on respirators; many, with heads swathed in bandages, had arms and legs in plaster casts. At least half a dozen had multiple rib fractures. Five had concussions. Byron Pulver, who had been trussed up in the back of Bouncer's pickup and thrown onto the highway in the midst of the pileup, had sustained the greatest trauma. Both his legs and arms were broken, his skull cracked, his pelvis fractured, and one lung punctured. On top of that, he was in a coma.

The Moosehead militia were two to a room and filled one entire floor of the tiny hospital. Cap, exhausted and sitting in a chair in the hall, was explaining to Hop Kesselman, the *Moosehead Herald*'s one reporter, what had happened earlier that evening.

"This bunch of boys here is a kind of unofficial fraternal organization. We were comin' from Buck Simpson's house where we held this year's annual meeting to decide on a cause to donate funds to. Like the boy scouts or Four H. We finished the meetin' and was headin' to town to listen to some music when—"

"Music?"

"Yeah, the Buster Butts band. That's some good music."

"It sure is."

"We was headin' to Moosehead when these trucks come outa the plains, just came roarin' into us. Man! You never seen nothin' like it. Racin' onto the road. BLAM! Hit us broadside! One right after another. Blam! Blam! Blam! Blam! An' we go spinnin' inta one another. Brakes squealin', metal slammin' inta metal, smoke pourin' out. I tell you! Man, that was a mess.

"An' their trucks! Heavy, steel-reinforced pickup trucks. Man, them Remos is crazy! Why do they want t' go around attacking people for?"

"How do you know it was the Remos?"

"They was screamin' 'Praise Jesus!" "Hallelujah" an' other stuff. They was screamin' in tongues an' had crosses painted on the doors of their pickups, an' fish signs. Man, I'm still shakin' when I picture them maniacs."

"That must have been terrifying."

"That is an understatement. I just pray the law catches them before they do this to some other folks."

"Do you mind if I take a few pictures?"

"Help yourself," Cap said.

Hop lifted the camera from around his neck. "What a story!" he muttered.

CHAPTER TWELVE

Inside CDC studios in midtown Manhattan, Brian Swiggert and Missy Woods sat on a couch on the set of CDC's morning news and entertainment program, "Wake Up, America." Swiggert was saying, "Welcome to the July Twenty-second edition of 'Wake Up, America.' We begin with live coverage of the standoff in Moosehead, Montana, where after an anxious night, the Remos continue to defy FBI agents, the Montana National Guard and local law enforcement."

"And later this morning," said Woods smiling, "we have a report on several controversial weight loss programs."

"And later in the hour," Swiggert resumed, "a dog training school that offers advice on keeping our dogs slim and trim. But first the news."

The news began with a brief story on the Moosehead standoff, then an equally brief report on the funeral for the recently assassinated French prime minister, followed by a fifteen second story on an emergency meeting of global finance ministers. Then Swiggert was back on the screen.

SWIGGERT: This morning we have with us the two men in charge of the Moosehead standoff—Colonel Amos Sledge, commander of the Montana National Guard, and J.T. Baker, Terrorism Response Chief of the Federal Bureau of Investigation.

The screen split with Swiggert on the left side and Sledge and Baker on right, side by side.

SWIGGERT: Good morning, gentlemen.

SLEDGE & BAKER: Good morning, Brian.

SWIGGERT: Mr. Baker, let's begin with you. Where do

things stand?

BAKER: This situation hasn't changed in the last six or seven hours. The terrorists are still bunkered inside their stronghold.

SWIGGERT: How much longer are you going to wait before taking action?

BAKER: They have approximately one hour left before we commence operations.

SLEDGE: We've given them every chance. They refuse to communicate.

SWIGGERT: I understand that you've brought two Apache helicopters to the scene—

SLEDGE: And one hundred National Guard troops.

SWIGGERT: There are some who are saying that is overkill.

SLEDGE: OVERkill!?

BAKER: These are terrorists!

SWIGGERT: Does it concern you that there are children in that house?

BAKER: Of course it concerns us—

SLEDGE: We don't know if the children are still there.

BAKER: It's up to the Remos to see that nothing happens to those children.

SLEDGE: We have to consider the danger this cult poses.

SWIGGERT: Gentlemen, thank you very much and the best of luck in this difficult situation.

SLEDGE & BAKER: Thank you.

Sledge and Baker disappeared from the screen.

SWIGGERT: CDC's Gus Harvey has been at this standoff from the very beginning.

Gus appeared on the split screen.

SWIGGERT: Gus, you've just heard Major-General Sledge and J.T. Baker, the FBI's terrorism response chief, say there's very little time for the Remos to surrender. Can you add anything to that?

HARVEY: The National Guard and the FBI have exhibited extraordinary patience in this situation. Especially in light of the fact that earlier this morning it was discovered that another party of Remos in a convoy ambushed and demolished a group of cars filled with local charity volunteers. They deliberately ran into them, causing serious injuries. The volunteers are now in a local hospital in critical condition.

SWIGGERT: Do we know where this other group of Remos is?

HARVEY: No one knows. They may have snuck into the Remos' compound. One of the locals says that he has seen a network of tunnels running for hundreds of yards leading to the house. But we have not yet verified that story.

SWIGGERT: So conceivably there could be a small army of Remos inside the stronghold.

HARVEY: That's correct. There's even a more frightening idea being circulated that the Remos may have escaped through the tunnels and are now actually surrounding the National Guard and FBI.

SWIGGERT: What kind of weaponry do the Remos have?

HARVEY: That's part of the problem. No one knows just how much armament they're carrying.

SWIGGERT: You traveled with them—followed them—for three weeks. In that time did you see any weapons?

HARVEY: No. But if they had the weapons—and J.T. Baker is saying they are heavily armed—they were obviously concealed.

SWIGGERT: We will stay with this very dramatic story as it unfolds. Gus, as always, our thanks.

2.

By seven-thirty all the women in the holding cell in Manhattan's forty-third precinct were sitting on their bunks. The redhead was smoking and talking to the pockmarked woman who had ordered Lorene to shut up.

"This is the third time they've stuck me here," said the red head. "The assholes love to hassle ya."

"I know whose ass I'm gonna kick if I find him alone," said

the pockmarked woman. "They ain't puttin' me here no more."

"Me neither," say the redhead. "That's for damn sure. Why don't they pick up the hookers?"

"The hookers is payin' em off," said the pockmarked woman.

"The pimps is payin' 'em off," said the redhead.

"Yeah, the pimps," the pockmarked woman agreed. "The pimps pay 'em off."

Neither Jeannie nor Lorene had spoken for hours, ever since the pockmarked woman had kicked Lorene. But now Jeannie had to say something.

"When are they gonna let us out?" she asked.

The redhead and the pockmarked woman looked at her.

"When they damn well feel like it," said the pockmarked woman and turned back to her cell mate.

An hour later Jeannie and Lorene were sitting in a shabby courtroom with dozens of down-on-their-luck defendents. After another hour the two women were lectured by the judge and fined $75.00 each.

Outside, Jeannie said, "Now we gotta make tracks to Lon's office."

3.

Ez Lawson and Alan Bird were sitting in their SUV parked on the shoulder of Highway X15 behind a long line of cars, a quarter mile from the Remos' former home. Lawson was on his cell phone, talking to his boss, Emerson Schuman, headquartered in an abandoned Miami warehouse.

Schuman was worried. "Your job," Schuman told Lawson, "is to make sure the FBI does not come out of this looking good."

"I don't know what we can do," Lawson said. "We tried, Mr. Schuman. We tried a diversion the other night to draw attention away from the standoff."

"You mean the arson job? Was that you two?"

"Yeah."

Schuman made a sound of disgust. "At the least, figure some way for the Guard to get the credit."

"Sir, Bird and I will think of something. I promise."

"Give it your best shot."

"We will, sir."

4.

At ten o'clock Lorene and Jeannie were drinking coffee in a luncheonette near the precinct station. By ten-o-ten they were in a subway heading to the southern end of Manhattan. At ten forty, tired and depressed, they were in an elevator on their way to Lon Jones' office on the fourteenth floor.

Lon Jones was in his early thirties, a member of one of Manhattan's up and coming law firms. Not yet a partner, Lon was ambitious and looking for the big case that would garner him national headlines. When Lorene called the day before and explained her grievance, he had wondered if hers was just another stab at quick money. But this morning one look at the *New York Times* had convinced him that she might have a case. An article on page ten by Rita Brockman related that the new *Grand Tally U.S. & World Atlas* had omitted the state of Montana, not only from the section of state maps but from the U.S. map itself. Lon learned that Grand Tally was suing its printer for screwing up and dropping the digital file for the map of Montana, and accusing the printer of redrawing the U.S. map. Further down, the article recounted the previous day's happenings on the "The Rex and Sally Lou Show." Lon had his secretary call the CDC network for a copy of yesterday's show, but she was told that they were unavailable. He sent her to buy a copy of the atlas.

When Jeannie and Lorene arrived at his office he gave Aunt Jeannie a hug and asked, "How was the trip?"

"Awful," Jeannie said.

"What happened?"

"It's a long story," said Lorene.

"Does your—shall we say 'lack of spirits'?— have anything to do with the news?"

"What news?" they asked.

Lon pushed the *New York Times* across his desk and pointed to a front page story with the headline: "Christian Cult Defies Law. FBI in Full Force at Montana Hideout."

The women pulled their chairs closer to the desk and read the story, and as they read Jeannie gasped, "Oh my God! That's right near us!"

"I heard 'a this bunch before," Lorene said. "I seen these Remos on TV. I had no idee that they was headed for Moosehead."

"A hunerd an' fifty FBI agents in Moosehead! Oh, Lord! I jus' hope Bouncer an' Buck don't hear about this."

"Course they're gonna hear about it," Lorene said. "They're probably out there right now."

"Oh, don't say that, Lorene. Please don't say that."

"Well, they'd have to be hermits not to've heard this story," Lon said. "It was the biggest item on the TV news last night."

The women looked at each other.

"And this story," Lon said, turning to page ten, "tells about the map and about a woman from Moosehead, Montana—you—who correctly answered a question that entitled her to compete for a Cadillac, but was shouted off the phone."

"Lemme see that!" Lorene said.

Lon pointed to the passage.

"Whaddaya know," Lorene said, "I made the *New York Times*. Now we got their butts."

"It's a very strange case," Lon said. "The mapmaker is blaming the printer for the mistake—which I personally don't believe—and the show's producer is claiming he thought the map was a gag." Looking at Lorene, Lon added, "I don't think there was any fraud intended. I think we're dealing with incompetence."

"What're you saying?" Lorene challenged. "That I don't have a case?"

"The show's producers have to give you a shot at the Cadillac. After the way those two hosts yelled at you—"

"That all? A shot at the Cadillac?"

"I don't think they intended to cheat you."

"Of course they did. How else would they come up with that stupid map?"

"I think Grand Tally screwed up and those TV people didn't know it and took their word that the map was good."

"So we'll sue Grand Tally too."

Lon shook his head. "They didn't try to cheat you."

"I know, but—"

Lon ignored her objection. "Right now I'll call the reporter who wrote this story," he said, jabbing his finger onto the paper. "I want her to interview you."

Lon pressed his intercom button. "Lisa, get me Rita Brockman at the *New York Times*."

"All right," Lisa replied.

A minute later Lon was on the phone, leaving Brockman a message.

Lon told the two women, "Call me in an hour."

5.

Lawson and Bird had driven several miles from the "standoff" to a deserted county road. There they opened a side door of their SUV and unlocked a leather bag. Lawson rummaged through it and pulled out Secret Service badges and identification given them by Schuman, who saw to it that each of his field agents had phony I.D.s from at least half a dozen federal agencies for emergency use. Then, opening two clothing bags and changing into clean clothes, the two men drove back to the roadblock.

There they were stopped by national guard soldiers carrying AK-47s.

Even as they approached, the guardsmen were waving them off and calling out, "You can't drive here! Turn around!"

Bird, who was driving, held his fake Secret Service I.D. out the window. He pulled alongside the guards.

"Secret Service," he said.

One of the guardsmen reached for Bird's wallet but Bird did not release it.

"Let me see it," the soldier said and Bird said, "You are seeing it."

The soldier, confused, turned to a comrade. "Do you know what the hell this is?"

The other soldier came closer and bent down to look.

Lawson popped out of the car. The soldiers straightened abruptly and pointed their rifles at him.

"Get back in the car."

Lawson, ignoring them, said, "Get the FBI over here! They'll know who we are."

The soldiers looked at each other and nodded. One of them said, "I'll get someone," and left.

A minute later Amos Brackston strode up.

"You're Secret Service?" he asked.

"That's right," Bird said.

Lawson held his I.D. in Brackston's face.

"Recognize it?" he asked.

Brackston, who did not want to admit he could not recognize Secret Service ID, stared hard as he tried to read it.

"Well?" Lawson asked.

"Yeah, Secret Service," Brackston said uneasily. "Yeah."

"All right," said Bird, "who's in charge?"

"J.T. Baker," Brackston said.

One of the National Guard shifted uneasily and said, "Colonel Sledge is in charge."

"Who's Sledge?" Lawson wanted to know.

"Head of the Montana National Guard," the soldier said.

"He's not in charge," Brackston said, "Baker is."

"Where's Baker?" Bird asked, and Brackston pointed.

"Where's General Sledge?" Lawson asked.

"He's on the other side of the house, in a clump of trees."

Brackston explained that seventy minutes ago J.T. Baker had given the Remos an ultimatum. Brackston explained that Baker was certain that Sledge intended to launch an assault without consulting him. If Sledge did that, he would get all the attention. Therefore Baker decided that his men would charge the house before Sledge knew what happened. Consequently

Baker had decided to begin the assault one-half hour ahead of schedule.

Bird and Lawson exchanged quick glances.

"Excuse us one moment," Lawson said to Brackston.

The two undercover agents walked several paces away.

"You talk to Baker," Lawson told Bird, "distract him, get him excited, get him pissed. Throw him off schedule. I'll go to Sledge and tell him what Baker's up to and get him to begin the attack."

"Okay," Bird agreed.

Lawson sprinted around the side of the house. Bird and Brackston walked to the small cluster of agents, including Siggy Harris, surrounding J.T. Baker.

"Mr. Baker," Brackston called out.

Baker turned.

"Mr. Baker," Lawson said, "I'm Tom Pickerell, Secret Service."

Lawson held out his fake badge.

"We're busy," Baker said, and looked away.

"What the hell is Secret Service doing here?" Harris asked Baker.

"Call this operation off," Lawson demanded. "The president wants this operation called off."

"Who the fuck are you?" Baker demanded. "Let's see some ID."

Lawson showed his badge again. "Mr. Baker," he said, "the president wants you to extend the deadline another twenty-four hours. It's a political decision."

"Political!?"

"The White House and Congress have been flooded with calls from people who think excessive force is being used."

"We haven't made a move!" Baker said.

"The president," Lawson said, "is addressing the nation on this standoff tonight."

"You're joking," Baker said.

"No," Lawson said, shaking his head. "No joke."

"I want somethin' on this besides your word," Baker responded.

"How'd you like a desk job?"Lawson asked.

Baker said nothing.

"I can arrange that," Lawson added.

Baker nodded his head.

"This administration is so fucked," Harris said to Baker.

6.

Lorene and Jeannie arrived anxious and out of breath at the marble entrance to CDC studios. As soon as they pushed through a revolving door into the art deco lobby, they saw a dark marble counter and a sign that read "tickets."

Moments later they were ushered to their seats in an auditorium filled mostly with middle-aged white women. Jelton stepped into the staging area.

"Welcome to 'The Rex and Sally Lou Show!' My, you all look relaxed. Are you're enjoying New York!!!???"

"Yes," some of the ladies murmured back.

"I didn't hear that! . . . Are you ENJOYING NEW YORK!!!???"

"YES!!!!"

"Very good. Now, before Rex and Sally Lou come out, I want to say a few things about the show. As you know, we're live, so you'll have to stay seated till the close. Today's format is not our usual. Instead of celebrity interviews, we've invited some ordinary people, like us. Only these people have a very sad story to tell. They all have relatives in the Christian cult now surrounded by the FBI and the Montana National Guard in Moosehead, Montana."

The audience gasped.

"Now . . . the success of each show depends very much on you, the audience. We need you to show your appreciation for our guests, so when you see John"—Jelton pointed to a stagehand with a cardboard sign with the word "APPLAUSE'" on it—"when you see John hold up that sign, please applaud enthusiastically. . . Now just sit back, relax, and enjoy the show."

Jelton looked at the director, who gave the "hi" sign and Jelton waved and walked off. The show's theme music started and a man with a microphone at the side of the stage said dramatically, "Now, from CDC studios in midtown Manhattan, it's 'The Rex and Sally Lou Show.'"

As piped music filled the auditorium, Rex and Sally Lou swept out from backstage, waving and smiling.

"Good morning!" Rex told the audience.

"How are you?" squealed Sally Lou.

"We've got a heck of a show today."

"We certainly do."

"Today," Rex said, "instead of our usual celebrity interviews, we feel the need to address a very serious and potentially dangerous situation in Moosehead, Montana. But before I introduce our guests, I want to apologize for what I thought was a gag on yesterday's show. Those of you who saw it, will recall a ridiculous map of the United States. It was ridiculous because it did not include the state of Montana. That map was drawn by Grand Tally, which calls itself The World's Foremost Mapmaker. Imagine!"

"Exactly," chimed in Sally Lou. "That map was stupid! No Montana! Duh!"

"It was such an obvious piece of junk that we"—pointing to Sally Lou and himself—"thought it was a joke."

Lorene's mouth fell open. She was about to blurt something out when she felt Jeannie gripping her arm.

Rex was still talking. "We understand that the situation in Moosehead has reached a critical stage; we've been told only minutes ago that the FBI and the Montana National Guard have issued an ultimatum to the Remos to come out within a half hour or else. Remember, there are children, innocent children, inside. Our prayers . . . are for a peaceful resolution.

"Here to help us understand the Remos' motives and to do what they can to resolve this horrible situation peacefully, are five of the Remos' relatives. We have asked them to speak directly to their loved ones, and we hope that the Remos, who may have a television set, are watching and will listen. Please welcome Stacey Dinkins."

The curtains parted and a very old, white haired black woman in a cotton print dress walked slowly out. The audience applauded wildly. When she had seated herself, Rex explained that Stacey Dinkins was the ninety-year-old mother of Charles "The Rock" Dinkins.

"Ms. Dinkins," Rex said, "it's obvious you're feeling enormous stress now that your son Charles is barricaded in that bunker. What can you tell us about him?"

"Charles is a good man. Worked hard all his life. Never got ahead."

"That's a shame," Rex sympathized.

"That's so unfair," Sally Lou agreed. "You work hard all your life and you don't get any breaks."

"I can't take much more of this bullshit," Lorene whispered to Jeannie.

"You and me both," Jeannie whispered back.

"What's Charles's story?" Rex asked Ms. Dinkins. "Where did he take the wrong turn?"

"Charles didn't take no wrong turns. I don't believe any of those people in that house done anythang wrong."

"House? What house?" Rex asked. "Are you referring to the bunker?"

"The house they all in. I seen all the videos of that so-called shootout, an' I didn't see nobody from that house with a gun!"

Rex was clearly taken aback. "Hold the thought, Ms. Dinkins. I'm going to introduce our next guests, Jedediah and Samantha Hudson."

The audience applauded loudly as the Hudsons walked onstage and Rex and Sally Lou shook their hands. They were long-boned Appalachians. Jedediah wore a suit that hung limply on his angular frame. His coat sleeves reached almost to his knuckles, and his trousers dropped over his shoes. He wore a wide stripped polyester tie. He had long sideburns and thinning hair slicked straight back. Samantha wore a robin's-egg-blue skirt and a green jacket. Her face was sallow and worn, like her husband's. They took a seat next to Ms. Dinkins.

Rex explained that Jedediah and Samantha Hudson were, respectively, brother and sister-in-law of Jed Hudson. "Mr. Hudson," Rex said, "tell us your thoughts on this terrible situation."

"I agree with what this lady said," Jedediah answered, nodding at Ms. Dinkins. "I didn't hear no shootin' comin' from the house, an' I didn't see no guns there neither."

"Them Remos wasn't shootin'," Samantha Hudson added. "The only shots that was fired had t'come from those FBI agents."

"Dat's right!" Ms. Dinkins said. "I think that fool shot his own toe off!"

As the audience began making rumbling noises, Lorene whispered to Jeannie, "Get ready to run down there, when I say go!"

"You think that FBI agent shot his own toe off!!!" Rex sounded flabbergasted.

"Yes, I do!" reiterated Ms. Dinkins.

"You think the FBI is lying about this?" Sally Lou asked.

"Of course they're lying!" Ms. Dinkins shot back.

Lorene jumped up and yelled, "They ain't the only liars!"

Everyone turned and looked at her.

"I'm from Montana an' I got somethin' to say about this!" Lorene said as she pulled on Jeannie's sleeve and started edging through the seats to the aisle. An usher blocked her at the last seat.

"Who is that woman?" Rex asked, perplexed.

Lorene heard him and called out, "I'm from Moosehead, Montana. Heard of that?!"

"Oh, my God!" Rex said.

"Remember Moosehead?"

"Of course."

"Yeah, from the state you said didn't exist."

"Are you really from there?"

"Yes."

"What a coincidence! Here we are doing a show on the siege at Moosehead!"

Rex was hoping he could turn this confrontation into an

added attraction.

"Go back to your seat now. A little later on I'll ask you some questions."

Mechanically, Lorene turned, and Jeannie turned, and they edged their way back to their seats.

Without missing a beat Rex announced to the audience: "And finally I want you to welcome our last guest, Georgina Willard."

Ms. Willard came on stage to applause and took her seat on the other side of Ms. Dinkins.

Georgina Willard, Rex explained, was George Slow Bear's sister.

"Ms. Willard," Rex said, "You and your brother are Lakota Sioux from Pine Ridge Reservation. But you don't live there anymore. You're a United Airlines employee."

"Yes, I am."

"And I understand you're a member of the Methodist Church."

"That is correct."

"But your brother is a member of this—I'm sorry if I'm offending anyone—this crazy cult. How did it happen? Where did George take a wrong turn?"

"George is caught between the white and Indian worlds. George is an alcoholic, and I think this cult offered him some simple answers."

Sally Lou looked heart broken and shook her head. "That's so sad," she said.

"It is," Rex agreed. He turned to a camera. "We'll be right back with more of this heartbreaking story. Stay tuned."

During the commercial break Lorene turned to Jeannie and said, "When they come back on the air, I'm makin' my move. No more talk."

"I'm right behind you, girl," Jeannie assured her.

When the show resumed, Sally Lou asked the guests if they had anything they would like to say directly to their family members.

Georgina Willard said, "George, come on out of there. The

day of the Sioux fighting warriors is over. Give yourself up. It doesn't make sense to die for nothing. I can help you get a job. You can stay with Louis and me until you get back on your feet."

"That's powerful stuff," Rex said, shaking his head. "Ms. Dinkins, is there anything you would like to say to your son Charles?"

"I don't think Charles or any of them is watchin' this show. Would you, if you was surrounded by hundreds of armed men with helicopters and armored veehicles? Would you? My son ain't no fool."

Samantha Hudson said, "The lady's right. No one in his right mind is goin' be be watchin' TV while he's about to be murdered."

"Murdered?!" Rex said in disbelief. "You think our government would murder innocent people?

Lorene whispered to Jeannie, "I'm makin' my move. You follow me after I get halfway down the aisle."

Lorene stood up again and began edging towards the aisle. The guests were arguing. The Hudsons and Ms. Dinkins were telling Georgina Willard that by begging her brother to step outside and surrender that she was tempting him to get himself killed.

"No wonder the Indians lost the wars," Ms. Dinkins snuffed.

Lorene had worked her way across her row to the aisle. An usher stepped up and whispered, "You'll have to stay seated till Rex calls you."

Sally Lou saw Lorene and said, "The lady from Moosehead wants to say something. Get her a microphone."

Someone ran to her with a mic.

"Can you tell us what's going on at the siege?" Rex queried.

"I sure can," Lorene said sweetly.

"Come on down!"

Lorene bounded onto the stage.

At that moment Jeannie began edging across the row towards the aisle.

"Who's that woman?" Rex sounded alarmed.

Lorene said, "My friend's from Moosehead."

"All right, let her come up."

Jeannie walked onto the stage as Rex stood.

"What's your name?" he asked Lorene.

"Alice."

"I'm Janice," Jeannie said, stepping forward.

A stagehand carried out two chairs. The other guests were staring at the women.

"Why the hell they bring them on?" Jedediah muttered to his wife.

"Before the break," Rex asked Lorene, "you jumped up and said, 'They're not the only liars!' Who were you accusing?"

Suddenly, sitting on stage with three cameras, Lorene realized that millions of people across America were looking at her. Rex had to repeat his question.

"You!" she said suddenly. "You and that skinny stick!" Lorene jumped to her feet, yelling, "Because yesterday you told the woman from Moosehead that she was a liar and that there wasn't no Moosehead."

Lorene felt she wasn't sticking up just for herself, but for all of Moosehead, which had been insulted by these New York smartalecks.

"I thought she was an ACTRESS!" Rex yelled back.

"I'm the woman you called a liar! I'm the woman from Moosehead!" Lorene yelled again. Then she ran at Rex.

Sally Lou began screaming. The Hudsons and Georgina Wilkins jumped up and backed away, but Ms. Dinkins was too stunned and too arthritic to move.

Just as Sally Lou screamed, Jeannie ran at her. Sally Lou stood and staggered backwards.

Rex was fending off Lorene's blows as Jeannie grabbed Sally Lou by the hair.

The audience was in confusion with people shouting and screaming. At that moment security guards swarmed onto the stage.

7.

Meanwhile, on the other side of the Remos' house, "secret service agent" Alan Bird was identifying himself to Colonel Sledge.

"Sir," Bird said, "the FBI is about to commence its attack."

"The attack is set for 0-200, ten minutes from now."

"Baker's abandoning the plan. His agents are going to storm the house."

Sledge was furious. "That SON OF A BITCH!" Sledge yelled. "Petrelli," he called to his adjutant. "Start the attack! Commence the attack!"

Pettrelli relayed the message to the helicopter pilots, the armored vehicle commanders, and the troop leaders. While the choppers swung down, the armored vehicles rumbled forward, firing as they came.The choppers came in low and fast over the house, firing scores of rockets into it. Simultaneously national guard troops began firing thousands of rounds into the house.

Within two minutes the Randall place burst into a giant fireball.

EPILOGUE

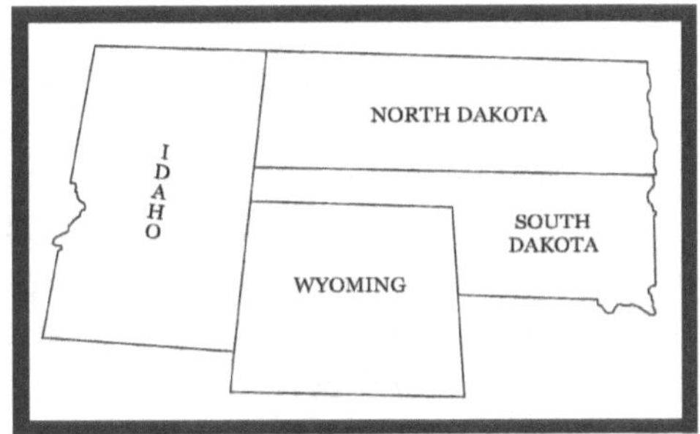

Shortly after the destruction of their one-time home, the Remos were apprehended and charged with twenty-one counts of attempted manslaughter, obstruction of justice, terrorism, and child abuse. The adults were tried amid a furor of national publicity and convicted on most counts and, to a person, received life imprisonment without possibility of parole. The harshest penalty was reserved for Reverand Angle, who was sent to the most dangerous cell block in the Montana State Penitentiary. As a result of God's failure to destroy the world, Reverend Angle lost his faith. He is now a pale ghost of what he once was, and works quietly in the license plate division of prison industries.

The Moosehead division of the Montana Militia, once they were released from the hospital, went back about their business of fearing government conspiracies. They are, however, no longer as active as they once were. Their serious injuries have not only confined several, including Byron Pulver, to wheelchairs but have dampened their spirits. Some of them still drink heavily, but they no longer roar around on gravel roads in pickups at ninety miles an hour at three-thirty a.m.

Others in this drama fared far better. Gus Harvey won a Pulitzer for his series, Siege in Montana, and is now the highest paid network journalist. He has signed a multi-million dollar contract with a New York publisher for a book on the tragic events.

FBI agents Kline and Harris testified before Congress and were commended for their work and promoted. Both received Presidential Medals of Freedom and offers of lucrative positions in private industry.

Lorene and Jeannie were arrested but thanks to Lon Jones's spirited defense, charges against them were dropped. (Both women had been hospitalized as a result of the fight.)

At first dismayed by the televised brawl, Jelton decided to play up the events, rather than try to cover them up or explain them away. He and the executives at CDC entered that show in the Emmys, and everyone connected with the program was overjoyed when "The Rex and Sally Lou Show" received Best Reality Episode of the Year. To capitalize on that windfall, Jelton offered Lorene and Jeannie large fees to appear on the show and reminisce about the entire affair. But the women had been devastated by the entire string of events and refused.

Grand Tally's resources were such that the printer pleaded for an out-of-court settlement, which stipulated that the printer create a free map for every disatisfied customer—one side delineating the correct contours of the continental United States and the other providing a map of Montana.

Several game makers cashed in on the Montana tragedy and produced computer games inspired by it. One computer simulation, "Death in Montana," became the top seller for that year. Its characters included the evil and demented Rev. Angle and his screaming tongue-twisted followers and their molested children; the heroic FBI agents Kline and Harris; the egomaniacal but tough no-nonsense J.T. Baker and his patriotic but friendly adversary, General Sledge.

The President of the United States moralized about the entire episode and drew lessons for all Americans. He praised the quick work of Homeland Security and the Montana National Guard. The fact that no one was present in the building when it was destroyed was not mentioned, nor did anyone ever use it to criticize the agency or the Guard. The press made no more than passing reference to it and therefore the public did not think to question it. Two months after the last newspaper headline on the tragedy, everyone in the nation, except the drama's principal players, had forgotten all about it.

www.ingramcontent.com/pod-product-compliance
Lightning Source LLC
Chambersburg PA
CBHW050448110726
47899CB00003B/856

* 9 7 8 0 9 7 4 1 8 2 6 3 6 *